DASTARDLY
DEEDS

DASTARDLY DEEDS

A SMITHWELL FAIRIES COZY MYSTERY

KARIN KAUFMAN

Winter Tree Books

"They say seeing is believing, but I can't tell you how wrong that is. It works the other way around."

~Ray Landry in *Dying to Remember*

CHAPTER 1

"**M**aybe I should explain what's going on," Angie Palmer said. She sniffed and ran a liver-spotted hand through her cropped gray hair.

Please don't, I thought. True, I'd been getting suspicious stares from Angie's friends since sitting down for afternoon tea in a brick-paved corner of her enormous greenhouse, but that suspicion would turn to anger if Angie revealed why she had invited me. But Angie was a no-nonsense woman in her sixties, and she preferred anger and hurt feelings to time wasted in useless speculation.

"Why don't we eat first?" I suggested. "I'll pour the tea."

"I suppose," Angie said. "There's always later."

Before she could change her mind, I grabbed the teapot. "Who wants tea? What kind of tea is it, Angie? It smells delicious. Where did you get it?" Angie knew me to be a tea aficionado, so she didn't find my questions odd, but Maya Estabrook seemed to realize I was stalling for time, and she didn't try to hide her incredulity. I could have planted corn in the furrows creasing her brow.

"What do you do for a living, Kate?" she asked, trying to uncover my purpose by approaching the matter from an employment angle.

"I retired ten years ago," I said. "My goodness it's warm in here."

Maya persisted. "Then what *did* you do?"

"I hope it's not too warm for you," Angie said, "but we do enjoy our twice monthly teas in the greenhouse. It seems an appropriate place to have them, even in summer."

"It's beautiful," I said. "I'd kill for a greenhouse like this."

"Don't let the butterflies land on your teacakes," said Harry Jelinek, the only male member of the Smithwell Garden Society in attendance. He needn't have gestured at the couple dozen blue butterflies flitting about our green metal table—especially above the jam bowl—but he did, as if I hadn't seen them. "Come in January, when it's snowing outside."

"Ah, yes," Angie said. "Yes, yes. December through February, really." She gave me a funny look, as though she'd just that moment decided against telling the group why I'd come. Too late. Maya was a bulldog.

"So what did you do *before* you retired?" she asked. "Your name is familiar."

"I worked here and there, Maya. I didn't really have a profession, but I still retired on my fortieth birthday, and now I garden a lot."

"Hence her visit," Angie said. With an unusual level of concentration for such a small task, she began to lather jam on her currant scone. She was a lousy liar. Too many tics and tells.

Maya took a cucumber sandwich and glanced around, no doubt looking for reinforcements. Who else was believing Angie's nonsense about my visit? I wasn't a member of the society, and except for Angie, whom I'd met several years earlier at a party, I was a stranger to the group. "Weird," she said. She took a petite bite of her sandwich. "I mean, why is your purpose such a secret?" She turned her large brown eyes on me.

"Stop being such a fidgety fuss and eat, Maya," Angie said. "The idea is to enjoy ourselves and soak in the summer. It won't be too long before we're wrapped in autumn gloom. Just look at the flowers, inside and out." Her strong Downeast accent, with its elongated vowels and Rs that went missing, commanded attention, regardless of the subject matter.

Harry swatted at a butterfly, the exertion of his movement almost popping a button on his too-tight shirt. I idly wondered if his beer belly got in the way when he gardened. Surely it must have. "Did you order more of these creatures, Angie?" he asked.

"Don't hurt them, for goodness' sake. And yes, I like my butterflies. I should have brought them a little bowl of fruit. They'd leave us alone then."

"You order butterflies?" I asked.

"You'd be surprised what you can buy online," she replied. "Caterpillars, chrysalises. I buy the caterpillars, though I collect them from my garden too. They have a lovely life in here. Longer and safer than they would outdoors."

Annabel Baker made a sour face. In her mid-thirties, she was the youngest of the group and the first to have introduced herself to me. She struck me as open and talkative, as rather obsessed with how her long dark hair cascaded in lush waves down her shoulders, and as somewhat sharp-tongued when she chose to be. "They don't have the home they were born into," she said. "They don't have freedom."

"Freedom?" Angie said. "Do you think they'll revolt? Overtake me in my bed at night?" She took a sip of tea. "Maybe I should set up sentries at the staircase. Or release birds in the greenhouse to prove my point about them having a longer life inside versus outside."

The sharp-tongued Annabel, realizing she was no match for Angie, sighed and changed tack. "Is the cress in these sandwiches from your garden? It's so fresh."

"Thank you. Yes, the watercress and the parsley are both from the backyard herb corner."

"Delicious."

At that we all fell silent, as if the six of us had simultaneously exhausted all possible conversational detours. The only sounds were cutlery on plates, a nearby fly or bee buzzing, and Harry's grunts as he tried to keep the butterflies at bay. When a lovely blue one parked itself on his shoulder, I had to bite back a grin.

But then I reminded myself that I had a job to do and that Angie was paying me in valuable orchids. I'd run into her a week earlier in the Hannaford supermarket, and there she'd told me about the thefts at her house and what she'd described as vandalism. The latter amounted to plant poisonings in her greenhouse and flower beds. After four months of meticulous inventory taking that she'd cross-referenced with her lists of members in attendance at Garden Society meetings, Angie had discovered what she'd suspected all along: the thefts had coincided with those meetings. I could have guessed that. Aside from her gardening acquaintances, my friend wasn't a sociable woman, so other visitors to her house were rare.

To make my job easier, Angie had invited only her suspects to this afternoon tea. Every single one of them had been present when something had been stolen or destroyed. The items taken ranged from old botanical books from Angie's voluminous library to small decorative ornaments from the library or greenhouse. These were not earth-shattering crimes, but finding the "betrayer," as Angie had put it, was important to her, and after reading how I'd helped the Smithwell Police solve a murder case on a birdwatching tour bus, she was convinced I could help.

But I wasn't convinced. Though I thought I might be able bring an unbiased eye to the thefts and vandalism since I'd never laid eyes on the suspects before. I might see or hear things Angie had overlooked. When she said she'd pay me in orchids for my opinion, I'd readily agreed. Decent orchids were expensive. The cheap ones I found in supermarkets always seem to die soon after I brought them home, and anyway, they weren't Minette's favorites by a long shot. She preferred terrestrial orchids—the cool-weather types that grew in forests—and Angie owned quite a collection of them.

So there I was, spying on Angie's friends so I could take a few orchids home to Minette, the four-inch fairy I'd discovered hiding under a terracotta pot last October. If one of my friends had told me that in the space of nine months my husband would die, I'd help solve a murder, and I'd find a fairy for a friend, I would have phoned the nearest mental hospital to carry him or her away.

"It's suddenly gone very quiet," Harry said.

"We're eating," Deborah Wetherbee replied. "And we're all wondering when Angie is going to spill the beans on Kate Brewer here. Obviously something's going on. Are you trying to bring someone else into the company?" Deborah gave Annabel a sidelong glance.

Annabel made a gagging sound. "No way. I'm next in line."

Angie clicked her tongue in reprimand, paused until she got the attention she wanted, then pointedly turned to me. "Kate, did I tell you that Deborah, Maya, Harry, and I created a natural products company using some ingredients from my garden? We call the company Ivy Cottage."

"We're not a conglomerate yet," Harry said with a grin, "but we're expanding. Right now we make an organic, beeswax-free lip balm, and this fall we're launching a hand cream and two natural oils. We have plans to hire three employees. Maya collects the ingredients, I'm the marketer, Angie is the financial backing, and Deborah is the master cook."

"The cheap labor," Deborah corrected.

"You know how to combine the ingredients," Harry said, "which is more than the rest of us do. It's a unique skill, and we're grateful."

"Do you sell your lip balm in town?" I asked.

"In five shops so far," Angie said, growing animated. "And we just obtained contracts in Rumford, Augusta, and Bangor. I can hardly believe it, but at sixty-three I have a brand-new career."

Maya tossed her honey-colored bob and puffed out her cheeks, making her already full, round face look like a pink balloon. "We'll give you a free sample, Kate, if you tell us what's going on between you and Angie," she said.

"Speak for yourself," Deborah said. "It's a lot of work to make a batch."

"And it stinks up your kitchen," Harry said. "We know, we know."

"I'll have a scone now," Angie said, sticking out her hand. "Plate, please."

Harry passed Angie the scone plate, and to avoid looking at Maya, I topped off my cup with more tea. I'd been in the greenhouse for twenty minutes and I hadn't learned anything of use about the people in front of me. Maybe Angie spilling the beans on my reason for being present wasn't such a bad idea. At least then we could get the ball rolling and I could ask some pertinent questions. For now, Maya and Deborah were stuck on who I was and why I was there, Harry wanted to swat the butterflies, and Annabel wanted to free them into the wilds of Smithwell, Maine.

"I brought back the book I borrowed," Harry said. "It's in the front hall in case you didn't see it."

"Thank you," Angie said. "Did you want to borrow another?"

"Your Gertrude Jekyll on country houses. And when I bring that back, your Lawrence Johnston."

"So you're studying the greats," Angie said.

Harry turned to me. "My wife and I are finally tackling the back garden—or should I say back yard? It's not a garden yet. But we want to start with a great master plan. What's your garden like?"

"Well, I've never had a master plan. I just find plants I like, plop them in the ground, tend them, and hope they do well."

Maya leaned forward. "I thought you liked to garden."

"She does," Angie snapped. "Not everyone gardens in the same way. We're not all Vita Sackville-West."

"Angie, why are you so sensitive today?" Deborah asked. "It's obvious something is bugging you. You're acting weird."

"Can't we finish our tea before you analyze me, Deborah? I want to show Kate what's new in my garden and library. Then to please Annabel we can all shout, 'Freedom!' as we release the greenhouse butterflies. How's that for a plan?"

"The second Kate walked in, you started acting like some scheme was taking shape," Deborah said. "Like you'd invited a conspirator, not a friend, to tea. We all read the paper, so we know how Kate gets involved in things—and I don't mean gardening. So what gives? You can tell us—we're all friends."

At the word *friends*, Angie bristled. "Are we?" She dropped her scone to her plate and brushed crumbs from her hands. "I'm taking Kate on a private tour. Maya, you can examine my calendula, and Harry, you can take a book from the library. Make it two. The rest of you"—she waved a hand—"explore the back and front gardens and let me have some privacy for a minute."

"All right," Maya said. "Sheesh galeesh. But you're not getting off that easy."

"I second that," Deborah said.

Angie's chair scraped along the brick pavers as she pushed away from the table and stood. "You want to know what gives, as you so eloquently put it? Do you really want to know?"

In my experience, Angie was like a tea kettle without a spout. She didn't vent—she exploded. "Maybe you could take me on that tour first," I said, rising from my seat. "Back here in fifteen minutes?"

She clenched her jaws.

"This way?" I walked off, drawing Angie away from her friends and whatever she'd been about to say to them. Once outside the greenhouse, I headed deeper into her back garden, waited for her to catch up, and turned.

"Friends," she sniped. "Deborah says we're friends."

"Most of you *are* friends," I replied. "Remember, it's probably only one of them, and there might be an innocent explanation for the thefts and plant poisonings."

Angie tilted her head and pursed her lips. "Please quit it. I'm not a child."

I shrugged. "We need to find a way to broach the subject without accusing anyone. You don't want to lose friends, and I don't want to make enemies."

"How on earth do we do that?"

"Good question. I'm beginning to realize I didn't think this through. We need a plan." Looking past Angie, I saw Harry and Annabel walking toward the house and Deborah and Maya exiting the greenhouse and veering off in different directions. A person could get lost in this back garden, I thought. Delightfully lost.

"I suppose you haven't picked up on much," Angie said.

"The only thing I've learned is that four of you are in business together and Harry is borrowing your books. Does he always ask before he takes a book?"

"Yes, and he takes one book at a time. At least I think so. I don't search him at the door, so who knows?"

"I doubt he's shoving books down his pants." I circled in place, taking in the grounds and feeling a major twinge of envy, though I'd seen her garden before. Two acres crowded with flowers, hedges, and fruit trees—and a greenhouse to boot. What I wouldn't have given. "Your back yard is magnificent."

Hearing a rhythmic rap on glass, I swung back to the house. Jack, Angie's husband, was at an upstairs window, banging on the pane so hard I thought he'd shatter it.

"Oh, Jack, Jack," she muttered, "you're supposed to be sleeping."

"Angie, he'll put his hand through—"

"He doesn't know what he's doing anymore." She rushed for the house, and I was left pondering her statement. Jack didn't know what he was doing? Now that I thought of it, I hadn't seen him in well over a year, and I hadn't asked Angie about him in all that time.

Seconds later, Jack disappeared from sight and the drapes fell back into place, and I supposed that Angie had called to him from the bottom of the stairs and warned him about breaking the window. Nimble as she was at her age, couldn't move *that* fast.

Deciding it would be rude to interfere by following her upstairs, I started my own tour of the garden, beginning with

Angie's white climbing roses, which sprawled over a waist-high stone wall that enclosed the grove of fruit trees.

A minute later, as I strolled through Angie's tiny grove of mature pears, I heard a scream that froze me in place.

CHAPTER 2

I ran from the fruit grove, my eyes darting left and right as I searched for the source of the scream. The garden? The greenhouse? I saw Maya running full tilt for the house and jogged after her, hoping her sense of sound direction was better than mine.

It *was*. I arrived in Angie's front room just behind Maya, and the scream, I quickly deduced, had come from Annabel Baker, who was now whimpering loudly. At her feet lay the bloodied body of Deborah Wetherbee.

I elbowed Harry aside and bent down.

"Is she gone?" he asked.

Deborah was sprawled like a rag doll at the foot of the stairs, her lifeless eyes staring at the ceiling. Blood had seeped from some unseen wound on her head, traveled in rivers down her face, and puddled on the oak-plank floor. Yes, she was gone. I didn't bother with a pulse.

"Someone call an ambulance," Angie said.

Out of habit, I dug into my jeans pocket for my phone before I realized I'd put it in my purse and my purse was in the greenhouse.

"No, no, I'll call," Angie said. "What am I saying? Don't anyone touch her."

She hurried off, probably for her kitchen, I thought. Angie was old school. She still had a land line there.

"I'm not sure, but I think her neck's broken," Harry said, his substantial abdomen making it difficult for him to bend close enough for a proper diagnosis.

I rose and asked everyone to move back and not touch anything.

Maya fixed her eyes on Annabel. "What happened?"

"How should *I* know?"

"You had to have seen something."

Annabel waved a helpless hand in Deborah's direction. "I saw the same thing you're seeing. She was like this when I came in. She must have fallen down the stairs and hit her head."

"What did you hear?" Maya asked.

"Kind of a thump. Not loud."

"I didn't hear anything until Annabel screamed," Harry said.

Though I doubted Annabel's theory about a fall, I said nothing. On second look, Deborah's wound appeared to be near the top of her head, a couple inches back from her hairline. She hadn't tripped and landed square on the top of her head. In any case, a fall down the stairs wasn't likely to result in the loss of so much blood, and there was nothing sharp or hard-edged on or near the stairs that she might have struck on her way down.

"What was she doing on the stairs in the first place?" Harry asked.

"Last time I saw her, she was walking toward the topiaries," Maya said. "She was ticked off about something but she wouldn't say what. Typical for her. Except she refused to come with me to see the *Calendula officinalis*, which was weird. She usually likes to examine it. I don't know where she went after that, but I was completely alone for two or three minutes."

Maya's account of her whereabouts contained an extraordinary amount of detail, I thought. I glanced about our small group. No one else seemed to have picked up om that.

"An ambulance is on the way," Angie announced as she returned. "And I've called the police."

Harry flinched. "The police?"

"Of course the police," Angie barked.

"Don't jump down my throat," Harry said. "It's not like I know the protocol for things like this."

"I know, I know." Angie massaged the bridge of her nose, walked over to the nearest chair, and slumped into it. "There was no need for the ambulance, was there?" she asked of no one in particular.

"It's always good to call one," I said. "The police would have if you hadn't. Let's all sit down. Can we use your kitchen, Angie? We shouldn't be in here. We need to protect the scene."

Annabel, who had finally stopped quaking, gave me a look of reproach. "The scene? You're in your element, aren't you?"

"Death isn't my element," I said. "I'm just using common sense. Your kitchen, Angie?"

"Of course," Angie said. "Let's go, everyone, please."

Giving Deborah's body a wide berth, Angie led us past her and into her kitchen the next room over. We all pulled out chairs and plopped down at her table. In the middle of the table, a blue butterfly—an escapee from the greenhouse—was roosting on a brown-spotted pear in a white ceramic bowl.

Harry pointed. "That's not sanitary, Angie."

"Because butterflies never touch fruit," Angie said. "Nor do bees or flies or ants. I do wash what I eat before I eat it, Harry."

"Are we focusing on insects to avoid the obvious?" Annabel said. She pushed her dark hair from her shoulders, gathered it, tugged it over her right shoulder, and flipped it back again.

The woman could not leave her hair alone. "What happened to Deborah?"

"Where did you go, Annabel?" Maya asked. "I lost sight of you."

"Are you accusing me?"

"No one's to blame," Harry said. "Obviously Deborah fell and hit her head."

Angie shot me a look. We both knew better than that. She'd invited me to solve cases of mere theft and vandalism, and now her genteel living room was a crime scene.

"Can I make coffee?" Maya asked. "I need something strong and tea doesn't cut it." Not waiting for an answer, she moved for Angie's coffeemaker.

"Anyone else?" Angie asked.

"Me too," Harry answered.

"And me," Annabel said.

Seconds later the sound of sirens rose above the clatter of coffee cups and spoons.

Angie got to her feet. "I'll show them where she is."

"We're going to be questioned," Annabel said softly.

That was a sure bet. There was one dead body and four clear suspects. Five if you counted Jack upstairs, and the police would do just that. I didn't include myself in that tally of course.

Angie headed for the front door, and Maya leveled her guns on me. "Let's be honest, okay? You investigate murders. I've read about you. You solved a murder on that birdwatching tour bus."

"I was in the wrong place at the wrong time," I said.

"The paper said you'd solved another murder too, before the tour bus. So why did Angie invite you?"

"We're old friends, and I've always liked gardening."

"Don't talk to me like I'm an idiot," she said through gritted teeth.

She was angry, and she conveyed that emotion by leaning my way and scrunching up her pink-balloon face. I'd never met Maya outside of Angie's house, but it was hard to take her and her bulldog act seriously. "You should talk to Angie. I'm not discussing her behind her back."

When Angie returned to the kitchen, she was followed by Detective Martin Rancourt and Officer David Bouchard. The Smithwell Police Department was a small force for a small town—population six thousand—and I'd met both men before. More than once, as a matter of fact. Rancourt's eyes shot my way. His shoulders drooped, he exhaled. *You again.*

"Officer Bouchard will take your statements, ladies and gentleman," he said curtly. "Stay here."

He exited the kitchen, presumably heading for the scene of the crime, where the medical examiner was probably already at work.

"Kate Brewer," Bouchard said, the hint of a smile playing on his lips.

"Yes, Officer."

"You."

"Yes, me."

"Let's start with you."

"Fine."

"Mrs. Palmer, we're going to conduct the interviews on your patio. Is that all right?"

"Absolutely, Officer," Angie replied.

Bouchard waved for me to follow him and then stepped out the kitchen's French doors. I considered Bouchard an adequately competent officer, but I also considered him a tad lazy. Thinking outside the box was not his strong suit, though his youth was largely to blame for that. He was a kid, really. Still in his twenties.

But he was, as far as I knew, an honest man, and I think Rancourt trusted him.

"Sit down," he said, motioning at one of the two wicker chairs on Angie's back patio. "I can't believe you're here."

"Neither can I."

"Since I don't consider you a suspect, let's—"

"Gee, thanks."

"Let's start from the top, before you found the body. You have a good eye and a good memory."

I told Bouchard about the tea get-together in the greenhouse, including why Angie had invited me, and I recounted as best I could the petty rivalries I sensed among the Garden Society members. Feeling a little like I was speaking out of turn, I also told him about Jack. "He's upstairs. I think something's wrong with him. Mentally, I mean. Maybe dementia, but you'd have to ask Angie about that."

"Who found the body?" He looked down at his notebook. "Of Deborah Wetherbee."

"Annabel Baker. She screamed, and that's the first I knew something was wrong. The only person I saw shortly after that was Maya. She ran for the house and I followed. Annabel, Angie, and Harry Jelinek were already inside."

"Did anyone touch Wetherbee?"

"Not after Maya and I entered. Before that, I don't know. Once Angie and I left the greenhouse, I lost track of where everyone else was."

"Did you see Jack Palmer downstairs?"

"No."

Bouchard jotted a few things in his notebook. The sun was bright on his face, spotlighting the freckles on his nose and cheeks. He put his notebook away and said, "Rancourt will want to speak with you later."

"I'm sure."

"How did you manage to get caught up in another murder?"

"How do you know it's murder?"

"I gave the body a once-over. It looks like someone struck her hard on top of her head. It doesn't look like an accident."

Since I'd come to the same conclusion, I simply shrugged and said, "Can I go?"

"Would you tell Angie Palmer to come outside?"

"Are you going to talk to Jack?"

"He was in the house, so yeah, I have to. Thanks for your help, and send in Mrs. Palmer. Let us know if you figure out who the thief is. Maybe it was Wetherbee and she was caught in the act."

"That's always possible." I headed back into the house through the French doors. In reality, I thought it unlikely that Wetherbee had been caught stealing. Angie was the only one who *might* react violently to catching a friend stealing from her house, but Angie had asked for my help to uncover the thief. She wanted to turn the miscreant in, to excommunicate her from her life, not kill her.

I let Angie know she was next, then went back to my seat, steeling myself for Maya's questions or accusations. But the moment Angie left the room, it was Harry who spoke up.

"Do they think Deborah fell?"

"No, Harry, they think she was murdered."

"That's absurd," he said, his voice rising in protest.

"It's not, and I think they're right. You saw her."

Annabel crossed her arms, hugging herself. "Deborah was murdered? It's unbelievable. Who could have . . . ?"

She didn't finish her question, but I knew what she'd been about to ask: Which one of them had killed her?

"Then someone pushed her down the stairs," Harry said flatly.

"It looks like someone hit her," I said. "Either at the bottom of the stairs or before she fell."

"What makes you an expert?" he said.

"Her expertise is why Angie invited her, Harry," Maya said.

Harry was dumbfounded. "Because Angie knew there'd be a murder?"

Maya rolled her eyes. "Of course she didn't know about Deborah. Who did? But Kate Brewer is here as a crime solver. Am I right, Kate? *That's* what you do. You're a wanna-be private investigator."

A wanna-be? I'd helped Rancourt on more than one murder case, truth be told, and he was beginning to value my opinion. Not welcome it, but find it of use. At age fifty, I'd found a new career—or it had found me. It's not as if I sought out murder scenes.

"What crime are we talking about?" Annabel asked. "You're not making sense, Maya."

"Ask Kate," Maya said.

And then it occurred to me that if Maya was the only one of the group who suspected I was at Angie's to solve a crime, then she also knew that a crime of some kind had been committed in Angie's house. And how, exactly, did she know that unless she'd committed that crime? "What crime do you think I'm solving, Maya?"

"How should I know?"

"You seem to know a lot."

"Only because I'm not stupid. I observe and speak the truth."

"If no crime has been committed, why do you think I'm here to solve a crime? Is there something you're not telling us?"

My amiable chat with Maya was interrupted by Jack calling for Angie and Rancourt commanding Jack to stay right where he was. I rose just as Angie, done with her interview, came back through the French doors, Bouchard behind her. "Jack's calling for you," I told her. I went after her, partly as moral support and partly to see Jack, and Bouchard trailed after me.

"Mrs. Palmer, stay right there," Rancourt ordered. He glared at me and I halted. Jack was at the top of the stairs, holding a pineapple-shaped ornament of some kind.

"He'll fall," Angie said. She circled Deborah's body and started up the stairs.

Rancourt grabbed her forearm. "Bouchard."

Taking the steps two at a time, Bouchard reached Jack and blocked a possible tumble down the staircase.

"But look at this," Jack said, raising the ornament. "This is out of place."

Bouchard was about to take the pineapple from Jack's hand when something caught his eye. "Sir," he said, looking over his shoulder at Rancourt, "we need an evidence bag. This thing has blood on it."

CHAPTER 3

"**M**y husband wouldn't hurt anyone," Angie said. "That detective—how dare he?" She was still steaming from her run-in with Rancourt, who admittedly wasn't the most tactful of men. "Jack's not capable, especially in his condition. But he never *was* capable." She grabbed Maya's now-cold left-over coffee and took a gulp. The others had left, the medical examiner had removed Deborah's body, and now it was just Jack upstairs and me and Angie at her kitchen table. I wanted to leave, but I decided to stay a little longer and try to reassure her.

Tears glistened in her eyes. Not only had a friend been murdered in her house, but to her mind, the police now considered her husband the prime suspect. At least that's how it had appeared to her when Rancourt had asked if Jack had any reason to want Deborah dead, and when he'd asked if Jack could distinguish right from wrong, and when he'd told Angie to bring him to the station for a fingerprint session. It didn't help matters any that Rancourt had found six spots of what appeared to be blood on the banister near the top of the stairs.

"He has dementia, maybe Alzheimer's," Angie said. "You don't become evil because your memory goes. He's still the sweetest man I know."

"The detective had to ask those questions. He wouldn't be doing his job if he didn't, and if he didn't do his job, any case he built against someone else would fall apart. That doesn't mean he thinks Jack did it. He's just covering the bases. I think he's trying to determine where everyone was when Deborah was killed."

"I guess so. I mean, if he'd killed Deborah he'd hardly be brandishing the murder weapon, right? How foolish would that be?"

Except that he's not in his right mind, Angie. I kept that contrary thought to myself.

"I'm glad he doesn't understand what's happening. He'd be offended. And scared. He gets scared easily."

"Angie, do you have help? You must need a break sometimes."

"A part-time nurse comes about six o'clock and stays the night so I can sleep. She's here all day on Saturdays, and sometimes during the week too. I thought this once, while we had tea, we could do without her. Jack had an early lunch and said he was tired. He fell asleep, but I should have hired her to come watch him, not left him alone upstairs while I partied in the greenhouse."

"Oh, Angie, it must be so hard."

"I'm all right for now. We're doing all right."

I was glad she had help, but it shocked me that Jack had gone downhill so rapidly in just a year and a half. The last time I'd seen him, he'd shown no evidence of dementia. But then what did I know? He must have been in the early stages at the time, probably trying to hide his advancing disease from outsiders.

"I promised you some orchids," Angie said.

"If I figured out who your culprit was, which I haven't yet."

"But still, let me make a down payment. Turns out I invited you to a murder instead, and that deserves a reward."

"Later," I said, laying a hand on her arm to keep her from leaving her seat. "I haven't given up on our theft case. We'll talk more. Tomorrow maybe? For tonight, try to get some rest."

"That nice Officer Bouchard mopped up the blood so I wouldn't have to."

"He's an okay guy."

I stayed to wash the coffee cups, said goodbye, then got in my Jeep.

On the drive back home, I reviewed what I knew about Angie's fellow society members. Not much that was concrete, I thought, but then again, I was beginning to grasp some of what made them tick, and that could be as useful in solving a crime as the bare facts.

I rolled the window down a few inches, letting the grass-scented air sweep over me. Clouds were starting to form, as they usually did on warm summer afternoons in central Maine, but the TV weatherman had put the chance of rain at only ten percent. I longed for a thunderstorm, a raging downpour, to wash away the heat and usher in cooler days.

With my mind focused on Deborah's murder, I found myself on Birch Street before I knew it. *My front garden isn't half bad*, I thought, pulling into my driveway. It was haphazard in its design and needed a late-summer sprucing up, but it was large and green and sloped lightly from my house on a hill down to the street. My view consisted of the woods across the way, but how perfect was that? Privacy, the bounty of nature in a large front yard. My envy of Angie's garden had faded to a speck by the time I'd parked in my dooryard.

I tossed my purse to the kitchen table and called for Minette. It was funny how much I missed her when I was gone for a few hours.

"Kate! Kate!"

A pink blur flew past me.

"What have you been up to?" I spun back. "Where are you?"

"On the refrigerator, silly."

"Very funny. You know my eyes can't keep up with you." She sat on top the fridge, her tiny legs dangling over the door. Though she looked dainty with her butterfly-like ivory and pink wings and shimmering light brown hair, Minette was capable of great speed, and she loved to tease me by calling to me and vanishing by the time I turned around. She was as fast as the ruby-throated hummingbirds that rocketed from feeders to the bright blue sky during a Maine summer.

"Kate, I've been waiting for you. I have to go to the Smithwell Forest."

"You can go. I need to rest." I sat, pushed my purse aside, and lowered my chin into my hands, still eyeing her. "Something awful happened at Angie Palmer's house."

She stood. "To you?"

"To a friend of Angie's."

Minette flapped her wings forward, went horizontal, and hurtled for the table. I shut my eyes—an involuntary reflex—and when I opened them, she was standing on my purse, her tiny bare feet making minuscule indents in the leather. "I'm glad it wasn't you, Kate."

"A woman named Deborah Wetherbee was murdered."

Minette squeaked and sat cross-legged on my purse. "We must investigate."

"I thought you'd say that."

"I see and hear things you don't."

"You've been very helpful in the past."

"Not just the past."

"I was going to surprise you, but Angie Palmer asked me to investigate some thefts and vandalism in her house, and she's going to pay me in orchids."

Her emerald eyes widened.

"The kind you like," I added. "Lady slippers."

"Then I must help you."

"We'll talk about it tonight, okay?" I leaned back in my chair.

"First . . ." Minette rose. "The Smithwell Forest."

Smithwell Forest was Minette's name for the woods across the street. Her full fairy name, in fact, was Minette Plummery of the Smithwell Forest, and at one time, she'd told me, her woods had been the home to other fairies, most of them good but many of them bad. But she'd never elaborated on that. How were these bad fairies bad? What had they done? I'd deduced that some sort of fairy war had taken place and that the good fairies had been driven from their homes in the trees, but that was the extent of what I either supposed or knew. Minette was reluctant to talk about it. It frightened her still, as if speaking about the great Smithwell fairy catastrophe could draw the ire of these bad fairies.

"We must go to the Smithwell Forest now," she insisted. She made fists with her hands. "We must because I need berries and I need to see my forest."

There was an urgency in her demeanor that I'd rarely seen, but I was tired and needed to sit and think. "Why can't you go yourself?"

"I can't. Kate, please." With one slow flap of her wings, she rose and drifted forward until her tiny face was inches from mine. "I can't go by myself. I'm too small."

"All right." Pressing my palms to the table, I stood. "Hide in my jeans pocket until we get far enough in the woods."

"But it's so tight in there."

"Gee, thanks. Slide halfway down and my shirt will hide the rest of you."

I left by my kitchen door and headed down my driveway, hoping I wouldn't see anyone who wanted to chat. My next-door neighbor, Emily MacKenzie, knew about Minette, but that was it, and I intended to keep it that way. Minette was not safe in a world where her existence was known.

Yet there was one other person who knew about Minette. He knew a great deal about the hidden fairy world, too, though he'd been coy about how he'd hit upon his strange expertise. Last winter, in spite of the police searching for him—he was wanted in a murder investigation—he'd disappeared, but I still looked for him whenever I went out. He was a ghost in the wind. Just thinking about Ignace Surette, a.k.a. Richard Comeau, sent tingles down my spine. He was evil. A weirdly obsequious man and almost certainly a killer, he would stop at nothing to capture Minette.

"I should have brought my walking stick," I said as we entered the woods. "What a tangle."

Minette wiggled out of my pocket, flew to my shoulder, and hid herself on my shoulder between my shirt collar and hair. Anyone with eyes could have spotted her because of the contrast: pink wings not quite hidden behind my brown-but-graying hair. "You must bring a walking stick next time, Kate."

"I will. You never know what you might bump into out here. A wild raccoon, a feral cat." *Or a crazed French Canadian obsessed with fairies.* "We're going to your tree first?"

"Yes."

"What are you hoping to find?"

"I'm hoping to find nothing." I felt her lean into my neck and grab fistfuls of my hair. "*Mmmm,*" she hummed. "I've got a . . ."

"Are you singing? That's a new one."

"*Mmmm*," she hummed again. And then, in a full-throated but sweetly tender voice, she sang, "Oh, I've got a brand-new pair of roller skates."

I stopped in my tracks. I didn't laugh, but only because I felt Minette, my brave warrior fairy, trembling against my skin. She was whistling past the graveyard—her graveyard being the forest—trying to distract herself from her fear in the only way she knew how. "I know that song. Where did you learn it?"

"Ray of the Forest liked it."

"Ray played that song?" My neighbor, Ray Landry, had been Minette's first caretaker of sorts. She'd stayed in his house on cold nights when she couldn't or wouldn't sleep in her forest home. Then, last October he'd been murdered. Soon after, I'd met Minette, and together we had helped find Ray's killer. I still missed him terribly. Time hadn't healed that wound.

Minette peeked out from under my hair. "You look sad."

"I never would have guessed that he liked that song."

"Melanie sang it."

"It's a nice song. The thing is, Minette, I didn't know Ray as well as I should have, or spend as much time with him as I should have, and it's too late now. So yes, that makes me sad."

"I'll sing it for you!"

Minette couldn't stand to see me sad, or angry, and she frequently commented on my emotional state, often chastising me for it. Though her concern was touching, keeping up a cheery front for her peace of mind could be tiring. "Don't sing. I'm fine."

"Oh, I've got a brand-new pair—"

"No, seriously."

"—of roller skates, you got—"

"Someone will hear you. Or hear me and think I'm talking to myself."

"Once more unto the breach, Kate."

"I've missed your Shakespeare quotes. All right, once more unto the breach. On to your tree."

"*Shhh.*" Minette pulled on my hair, hard enough to hurt, and I felt her scoot around the inside of my shirt collar until she was at the back of my neck. "Badness," she whispered.

Her hearing was phenomenal. I knew that. So although I didn't hear or see anything out of the ordinary, I stayed rooted in place and kept my mouth shut. There was danger out there. If not for me, then for her.

CHAPTER 4

When I could stand it no longer—literally, because my leg muscles needed to *move*—I begged Minette to tell me what she was seeing or hearing. When she didn't answer, I asked, "Is it a person? Please tell me it's not that Surette monster. I was just thinking about him."

"It's not the Ignace Surette," she answered in a barely audible voice.

"Bad fairies?"

Minette let out a plaintive peep.

"This is crazy." I turned slowly in place, searching every tree and shrub in sight. Madness. There were fairies out there? I felt as though I had crossed an invisible boundary and entered a storybook world—and not a pleasant one. This was the dark forest, full of foreboding, a place of red hoods and wolves, of wicked children gobbled by old crones. "Is this why you wanted to come here?"

"I heard them yesterday, but I ran away," Minette said softly. "More of them are coming, and they must not."

"You're safe with me, I promise. But you're going to tell me what happened in this forest between the bad and good fairies. I can't help you if you keep secrets."

"Yes."

"And if anyone tries to hurt you," I shouted in my most threatening voice, "they won't survive five seconds."

A fly buzzed past my ear and a gust of wind set maples leaves dancing. It was a beautiful late summer day, that's all. A peaceful day in the woods across from my ordinary house on Birch Street. I had just about talked myself into believing that everything I was seeing and hearing was part of the natural, normal world when something green plunged from the sky and dove for my face at such speed it almost knocked me off my feet.

I screamed and threw out my hands, but as swiftly as it had come, it was gone. Minette began to crawl up my neck and into my hair, but I was angry and ready for a fight.

Of course I was ready. I was five feet seven and she was all of four inches. Four terrified inches. "Calm down, Minette. You want to keep them out of your woods, don't you?"

"Yes, Kate."

I took a deep breath. What in heaven's name was going on here? This was pure insanity. I felt like I was tumbling down the rabbit hole. My late husband, Michael, had often told me I let my imagination run wild, yet he never could have guessed at *this*. "Did you see it? It was a bird, right? A parakeet, maybe. Someone lost a pet."

"No."

"A blur of bright green. That's all I saw—a bright, shiny green. Tell me it wasn't a fairy."

"It was Hacquetia. We must go home and I'll tell you."

"Hacquetia? You know it?"

"Her."

Now my heart was racing. "Unbelievable." I heard something slither behind me. A harmless snake, probably. There were small snakes in the woods. Big black flies, foxes, salamanders. Fairies. "How many bad fairies are there?"

"Too many."

"Do you want to check on your tree?"

"No, Kate, they're everywhere. I hear them."

"This is unreal. It isn't happening." I took another deep breath, turned toward Birch Street, and got out of there as quickly as I could.

When I hit the bottom of my driveway, I wheeled back with my fists flailing, sure I'd been followed by Hacquetia—and ready to strike her down. I must have looked like a lunatic, because the very next second my neighbor Emily called to me.

She was dead-heading roses on her front lawn and looked as if she'd gone stiff at the sight of me. "Come to my house right away," I shouted as I ran up my drive.

I flung myself through my side door, collapsed into a kitchen chair, and told Minette to let go of my neck.

"Hacquetia is bad," she said, fluttering to the hutch.

"I gathered that. She flew right at my face."

"She leads the bad ones."

"Great. I met the leader, did I?"

When the doorbell rang, I ordered Minette to stay where she was and prepare herself to shed her coyness and *talk*.

Emily was on my front steps, still holding her garden shears. "You're not going to believe this," I said. "Is Laurence home?"

"Not for another two hours."

"Good." I seized her shirt sleeve and dragged her to my kitchen. "Have a seat. Minette and I were just in the woods."

"Didn't you have a tea party to go to?"

"I did that earlier, at Angie Palmer's house. Deborah Wetherbee was murdered there." I sat and pointed to the chair across from mine. "But first the woods."

"Huh? Are you serious? Deborah Wetherbee?"

"Something just happened to me in the woods." Poor Emily. I had upended her world by introducing her to Minette, and now I was going to tell her about evil fairies converging on our woods, assembling for . . . what? Battle? "Minette, please come to the table."

Sitting cross-legged next to her teacup, she shook her head and refused to look at me. "Maybe later, Kate. Can I have some syrup? I'm *starving*."

"No, you will *not* avoid the subject. Not after what happened to me."

Her chin quivered.

"Come here, please. Emily and I are going to help you."

She looked at me, this time with a touch of hope in her green eyes. Maybe mentioning Emily had turned the tide. It wasn't going to be feeble old Kate on her own.

"I'll always help you, Minette," Emily said. "No matter what. You know that."

Minette thrust out her arms, like a swimmer about to dive, but then flit halfheartedly for the table.

"Tell us what happened in those woods and when," I said after she sat. "I mean when Hacquetia took over."

"My parents and friends . . ." Minette's expression was pitiful, beseeching. I was asking her to do something inexpressibly hard, but I saw no way around it.

Curiosity wasn't the main thing driving me. First and foremost, I cared for her safety. "Wait a second. It just occurred to me. I know the fireplace flue is closed, but is there any other place a fairy could enter this house?"

Emily gave a tiny gasp. "Another fairy? What?"

"I could never find another way to get inside," Minette answered. "It's safe."

"Good. When did the bad fairies take over the woods?"

"Bad fairies?" Emily raked her fingers through her short, copper-colored hair. "That sounds like an oxymoron."

I held out my hand palm upward, laid it on the table, and invited Minette to sit on it. "When did Olc happen?"

Her eyes grew wide as she clambered onto my hand.

"I read the word in Ray's journal," I continued. "Remember I read you part of his journal? You spelled the word for him. He said you called that time of chaos and death in the forest Olc."

She nodded.

"I still have Ray's journal, but he didn't write down everything and you didn't tell him everything. When did Olc happen?"

"The summer before I met Ray of the Forest."

"So two summers ago? Two years?"

"Yes, Kate."

"Ray wrote that fairies were driven out of the woods, even killed."

Tears began to fill Minette's eyes. "My family died."

"Oh, Minette, what happened? *Why* did it happen?"

She brushed away her tears. "Why does it surprise you that there are bad fairies? Badness is everywhere. There will *always* be bad fairies and bad people and bad everything."

I glanced at Emily. She'd clamped a hand over her mouth and was staring at Minette, obviously flabbergasted by what she was hearing.

"How did Olc start?" I asked.

"Hacquetia and her friends thought they were better than all other fairies, and they wanted the forest for themselves. They said the Smithwell Forest was too small for everyone. They didn't like humans in it either, and they wanted to make it look haunted to scare the humans away."

"How many fairies are we talking about? Before Olc, I mean."

"Seventy-six."

I flopped back in my chair. "Good heavens. Seventy-six fairies in the woods across the street? All this time?"

"They died or left, Kate. I left too when I met Ray. I was alone and . . ." Minette latched onto my thumb, climbed down from my open hand, and stood on the table. "I was afraid."

Astonishingly, she looked ashamed of her fear, as though she should have stayed in the forest come what may, even if it meant her own death. "I'm glad you left and found Ray," I said. "And I know he was glad too. If you hadn't left, who knows what might have happened to you? You made Ray's final months very happy."

"But I lost my forest."

"Sometimes it's wiser to leave."

"To *run away*, Kate."

"Yes, run away. Then you wait, regroup, and retake what's yours. And that's what we're going to do, Minette."

Emily found her voice. "Holy guacamole. A war. Who knew all that was going on across the street? I never, ever saw a fairy—or heard one."

"Our homes are high in the trees," Minette said. "Not on the ground like some people think."

"But still . . . holy guacamole."

I could tell Emily was struggling to wrap her mind around it all. To tell the truth, so was I. One fairy in the Smithwell woods? Okay, I'd come to grips with that. But once upon a time there had been dozens? Minette had told me there were fairies all over Maine. And not just Maine, but New England, the United States, the world. Did that amount to *millions* of fairies? Once again Minette had turned my happily settled view of the world topsy-turvy.

But back to the business at hand. I didn't like this Hacquetia, and I was going to see to it that *she* was driven from the woods. "Tell me what you know about Hacquetia."

"I know many things, Kate. I know Hacquetia is *greedy*." She loaded that final word with as much venom as I'd ever heard in her sweet, high-pitched voice.

"How did she start Olc?"

"She killed my friend Pirabelle."

Minette turned away from me and started walking across the table toward the window. "Can I have maple syrup now?"

My tiny friend, this fifty-seven-year-old fairy with the face of a child, was a paradox. Alternately as wise as a loving grandmother and as transparent as a toddler. I urged her to tell me more about Pirabelle and Olc, but she wouldn't, and I didn't want to press her in front of Emily. "We'll talk more tonight. And then we'll make plans. You're going to have your forest again."

Keeping her back to me, Minette started to hum. I looked at Emily and shook my head. "I think we need some maple syrup."

"Got tea?" Emily asked. "Tell me about Deborah Wetherbee."

The humming ceased and Minette turned around. "Olc brought the humans with nets and birdcages."

"To capture fairies?" I asked.

Emily gasped.

"Ray mentioned that in his journal too," I said. "I wouldn't be surprised if Ignace Surette wasn't drawn to the woods by all that activity. A former government agent who dabbles in, let's say, the unusual side of life would have his sources. Or maybe he happened to be in the woods and knew what to look and listen for in his hunt for fairies."

"But you and Michael foraged for blueberries in those woods," Emily said. "Did you ever see fairies or sense that they were around you?"

"No, but we weren't thinking about them, and we sure weren't looking for them. I didn't believe they existed, and so they didn't. I never gave them a thought. If I heard rustling in the trees above, it was the wind or a squirrel. If we *had* seen a fairy, we would've talked ourselves out of it, just like Minette says humans do. Even today, when Hacquetia dove for my face, I told myself she was a parakeet, of all things."

"She dove at you? She's a nasty little beast, isn't she, Minette?"

Minette opened her mouth to reply but was interrupted by my phone ringing inside my purse. I dug it out and was surprised to see Annabel Baker's name on the screen.

"Annabel, hi." The first question that popped into my mind was *Why on earth are you calling me, a stranger, hours after your friend died?* Thinking that would be a little brusque, I asked, "Is everything all right?"

She told me she had something important to tell me about Deborah and we had to meet.

"How about my house in ten minutes?" I said. The idea was to distract Minette from her sorrows by getting her involved in another murder investigation. How she loved to play private detective.

"Sounds good," Annabel said. "That way none of them will see us talking. See you in ten."

CHAPTER 5

Annabel fidgeted in my kitchen chair. I had made her coffee—I kept a bottle of the instant stuff in a cabinet for the unexpected coffee-loving visitor—but she hadn't tasted it. She'd played with the cup handle and she'd jiggled her right leg as though she had to make a bathroom stop, but she hadn't breathed a word. I shot a glance at the hutch. Minette was hiding in her Wedgwood teacup, and thus far she'd followed my instructions to stay below the cup rim and out of sight.

Emily had considered hiding herself—in my living room, not in a teacup—and had agreed to leave the house only if I promised to tell her what Annabel said within two minutes of the woman driving away. So far Annabel had not coughed up any goods. When I sat across from her with my freshly made cup of almond oolong, I figured it was time to force the issue. "What's bothering you, Annabel?"

"Before I tell you, can you answer a question for me? Why did Angie invite you to the tea meeting? I need to know."

"I'm not sure I can tell you that." I took a quick sip of my tea. "It's for Angie to say."

"It's just that . . ." She looked down at her hands and then out the window before she turned back to me. "Okay. Well, I think I know why she did, because I know something. And the thing is, it might be related to Deborah's murder. Or no, no." She waved her hands as if to physically erase what she'd just said. "It's *not* related, but people might think it is, and that worries me."

"Have you talked to the police?"

"My dad always says you shouldn't volunteer information to the police, especially if you've done nothing wrong but maybe you kind of, well, look like you did. Sometimes it's best to keep your lips zipped. Know what I mean?"

Yet here she was, supposedly to tell me something about Deborah. Was she ever going to get to the point? I pressed her. "I can't help if you don't open up."

She cradled her coffee cup and studied my face for a good few seconds. Then, having decided in favor of trusting me, or figuring she had no choice, she exhaled and plunged ahead. "I think you were at Angie's house to find out who's been taking some of her things. Am I right?"

I didn't answer.

"You've never come to one of our meetings before. You're a detective, and detectives detect crimes."

"I'm not a detective."

"So like you said, you were in the wrong place at the wrong time when you solved that murder on a tour bus, and today when Deborah was killed, but you do help the police. Would you *please* tell me if I'm on the right track?"

"You're not on the wrong one."

Annabel's shoulders drooped. "I think I'm one of the reasons you were there. The thing is, I've taken some stuff from Angie's house lately. Kind of in compensation. That's how I look at it."

She paused, trying to get a bead, I think, on what I was feeling. Was I outraged? Would I run to Angie? I kept my expression neutral.

"I've been left out," she went on. "Angie and the others—they're starting to make money from Ivy Cottage. They said they might hire me as an employee soon, but they won't make me an officer and shareholder like they are. They never considered me, Kate. I wasn't invited, and I hate my dead-end job at the Town Office. They all know that."

"Okay, I see," I said flatly. It was as noncommittal as a response got, but I needed Annabel to keep talking.

She clutched a thick strand of her dark hair and twisted it in her hands. "You didn't know about the company when Angie brought it up, I could tell. Deborah was trying to get my goat when she asked if you were going to join Ivy Cottage. Wasn't she?"

"Maybe she really thought that Angie was looking to bring—"

"Then I was right to be angry. They're planning to bring someone else in instead of *me*."

"Could it be that they haven't asked you to be a company officer because you're younger?"

"I'm thirty-one. Not a kid."

"I understand, but maybe they think you don't have enough business experience *yet*." I didn't want her to clam up, so I made a point of emphasizing that matters might change and in the future the others might well invite her to join the company.

Annabel disagreed. "None of them have any business experience. Harry's done some marketing, but the others—what do they know about starting a natural products company? Not a thing. They wanted to limit the number of people splitting the profits, that's all."

"You may be right, and I can see how you'd feel left out. But as you rightly pointed out, I don't know anything about the company. Let's get back to your compensation. What did you take?"

Annabel chewed on her lower lip. "That's . . ." She grunted and exhaled and toyed with her cup handle. "That's why I'm here. I took pineapple ornaments from the library. She has so many of them, and they're pretty, and I wanted a few so I could paint a patina on them, like verdigris."

"And you know Jack found one of those ornaments with blood on it."

"Yeah, I saw you two run out of the kitchen, and I asked Angie what happened before I left the house. It's almost like someone is trying to set me up. Why would they use a pineapple ornament to kill Deborah? I don't know what to do. If I tell the police, I'm admitting I took the ornaments. And the worst thing is . . ." She grunted and whined at the same time, as if she had a massive case of indigestion. "The thing is, today Deborah saw me take one from the library and put it in my purse. She said she wasn't going to 'let it go'—her words. Then I saw her talk to Maya."

"Did she tell Maya about the ornament?"

"I think so, but I'm not sure."

"Did Maya say anything to you after that?"

"No, but she will. Maya likes to collect secrets and use them when she needs them. Now I'm wondering if she'll tell the police."

I heard the fear in Annabel's voice. Was it because she might be wrongly accused of murder? In Rancourt's eyes, being caught in the act of stealing would be sufficient motive. People killed for all sorts of small and stupid reasons. Maybe Annabel had panicked and silenced Deborah with a whack to the head. But if that were true, why would she be telling *me* about the ornament? And anyway, if Deborah had told Maya about the theft, killing Deborah wouldn't have assured that Annabel's secret stayed a secret. She knew Maya could tell on her as easily as Deborah might have.

"How sure are you that Deborah told Maya you took the ornament?" I asked.

Annabel thought a moment. "Pretty sure, but not positive."

Buying myself time to think, I rose and took my teacup to the sink to rinse it out. That Maya also knew about the ornament, and that Annabel was now telling *me* about it, seemed to argue against Annabel being the killer. It made no sense for her to silence Deborah but not Maya. Or me. Still, I couldn't shake the feeling that she wasn't being entirely forthright and that she was using me as a pipeline to the police for her own purposes. She knew I'd talk to Rancourt eventually, seeing as how the local newspaper had painted me as an amateur detective, and confessing that Deborah had caught her in the act of stealing made her look innocent. By talking to me, she was making a preemptive strike.

I leaned against the sink and watched her briefly, looking for tells and tics. She was absentmindedly stroking her hair, but as I'd learned on first meeting her, she frequently did that. "Who do you think killed Deborah?"

The question threw her off balance. "Wow, me? How should I know? I was as shocked as anyone, and not only because I found her. She was one-fourth of Ivy Cottage, and the only ingredient cooker and mixer."

We were back to the lip balm company. "The 'cheap labor' is how she put it."

"No one wants to take on the mess it made in her kitchen. Harry always praised her for knowing how to mix the ingredients, but that was so she'd keep doing it and not complain. Why would they kill her?"

"Could anyone take over Deborah's job?"

Annabel considered. "Yeah, but you could say the same about Maya's and Angie's jobs. Though Angie's the one with the bucks. Harry's the only one who brings any real expertise to the group, and it's not much."

"What about Jack?"

Annabel dropped her hair. "Huh?"

Had I knocked the wind out of her? "Do you know if Jack and Deborah got along?"

Recovering quickly, she replied, "Jack gets along with everyone."

"Angie told me about his dementia."

"Jack gets prickly when he's confused, but he's not outright mean. But before he was . . ."

I urged her on. "Before he was diagnosed?"

"Yeah. He and Deborah didn't get along great. No, that's not putting it right. He got along with her well enough, but *she* didn't like being around *him* when he came downstairs. There was bad blood."

"What about?"

"I don't know. Something must have happened before I came along, but with Jack losing his memory, it wasn't an issue to him."

"Could Jack hurt someone without knowing the damage he was doing?" How far gone was Jack in his dementia? That's what I wanted to know, and I wasn't sure I'd get the truth from Angie, who was probably kidding herself about his mental health.

"I never saw him hit Angie or anyone else," Annabel said, "but the last time I said more than hi to him was three months ago. I could tell his condition was a lot worse, though he seemed very happy in spite of it all. Kind of oblivious but cheerful, you know? He didn't remember who I was, but he smiled at me and the others, and Angie cut him a slice of banana pound cake—that's his favorite. He grinned like a kid while he was eating it, then he said he was sleepy and went upstairs for a nap."

"Did he go up on his own?"

"Angie followed behind him to make sure he didn't fall. These days Jack doesn't come down to the first floor much, though he's not unsteady, you know? He gets around okay. Angie's talked about putting a gate at the top of the stairs or moving his bedroom into the living room, but she says he'd find a way to open the gate or try to go over it."

I heard a tap on porcelain but ignored it.

"Do you have mice?" Annabel asked, her eyes wandering over the kitchen.

"It's probably a fly knocking into things." *Or an impatient fairy in my hutch.*

"That's some monster fly, but they grow them big in Maine."

"Black flies hitting a light bulb make a weirdly loud sound. So do moths." Before I could regale her with other insect stories, the doorbell rang. "Excuse me."

I'd been so engrossed in my conversation with Annabel that I hadn't heard a car pull up my driveway. With her exceptional hearing, Minette had, and she loved to show off by playing I Know Who the Visitor Is. This time it was Detective Rancourt at my door. Annabel was going to freak.

I invited the detective inside, told him I had a guest, and led him to the kitchen. Annabel's jaw dropped.

"Annabel, you know Detective Rancourt."

"Huh, yeah."

"Detective, Annabel just stopped by to say hello." I wasn't going to do Annabel's job for her by passing along her information. At least not in front of her. I assumed I'd need to talk to her again and I didn't want to lose her trust by ratting on her in her presence.

"Good afternoon, ma'am," Rancourt said.

"Same to you," Annabel said. "I need to go, Kate. Thanks for the coffee."

She hadn't touched it, but then there weren't many drinks less appealing than instant coffee, and my bottle of it was two years old. I knew that because I'd purchased it about six months before Michael's death, and I timed a lot of things in my life by that benchmark.

"Don't go on my account," Rancourt said.

"No, it's getting late, and I have to stop at the grocery and go home and get dinner started and, you know, that kind of thing."

"I parked in the turnaround so you can get out," the detective said.

Annabel double-timed it out of my house and slammed my door on her way out, two facts that didn't escape Rancourt's notice. He settled his hefty frame into a kitchen chair. "I take it she wasn't here just to say hello."

CHAPTER 6

Looking as pasty and haggard as ever, Rancourt rubbed his
eyes. "Are you going to tell me what she had to say? Save
me some time?"

I sat down. Of course I was. We had become cordial, if not
outright friendly, and I knew he talked to me—said things to
me—that he didn't to other members of the general public.
In short, he trusted me. In return, I considered him a man of
integrity and a first-rate detective. His was a sharp mind inside
a fifty-something, junk-food-eating body.

"It's possible she wanted me to tell you what she told me. I
can't figure out how much of what she said was the truth or
was calculated to make her look innocent."

"Let me decide that."

And occasionally Rancourt felt the need to remind me that I
was an amateur.

I filled him in on everything Annabel had told me in our
abbreviated conversation. As I finished with "She doesn't know
if Deborah snitched on her about the pineapple ornament," the
phone rang. It was Emily. She'd seen Annabel's car maneuver
around Rancourt's SUV and speed off down Birch Street. Why
was the detective at my house? I answered her question with an
invitation to dinner. I knew she'd planned to have dinner with

her husband, Laurence, but she got my drift: I couldn't talk until Rancourt left.

"So, Detective, what brings you to my house?" I asked when I returned to my chair. Keeping in mind that Minette was still squirreled away in her teacup and growing restless, I didn't offer him coffee. Rancourt was no fool and wouldn't buy my stories about flies and moths striking light fixtures.

"Tell me more about the thefts and vandalism at Mrs. Palmer's house. Any suspicions on who was involved?"

"Aside from Annabel, none, really. Harry Jelinek likes Angie's books, and books have been stolen, but Angie said he asks to borrow them. We know now that Annabel has taken ornaments from the library, but she might not be the only one. Angie told me she's missing teacups and utensils too. I never saw evidence of the vandalism. Oh, and Angie said some of the potted plants in her greenhouse were poisoned."

"How?"

"She thinks someone used an herbicide. Since the plants shriveled and turned brown overnight, she ruled out a disease and ruled in a fast-acting weed killer."

"Did she have these plants tested?"

"No. It was only after the second incident that she considered their deaths were deliberate."

"So she invited you to her house to see if you could pick up on any clues she'd missed?"

I shrugged. "She's a friend, I thought it couldn't hurt to listen in, and she was giving me some orchids in payment. Why not try to help? For all I know, every one of those people was stealing from her."

"The troubles at her house don't have to be connected to the homicide."

"Agreed. Maya knew from the start why I was there. She told everyone I'd come as a 'crime solver.'"

"Interesting."

"She knew crimes had been committed at the house—or possibly somewhere else, but involving one of the society members present. That means she's either involved in the crimes or knows someone in the group who is."

Rancourt seemed skeptical. "You're getting ahead of yourself."

I raised my hands, granting his point. "Or she read about me in the papers, jumped to a conclusion, and wanted to show the others how clever she is."

"You don't like her."

"She's not easy to like. That doesn't make her a killer."

"What do you think of Annabel Baker?"

"Her coming to see me might have been a preemptive move. She thinks Maya knows about the pineapple ornament she put in her purse and believes Maya will eventually tell you. Annabel was also the first to find Deborah. Was that also a preemptive move? She screamed like a banshee."

"Wouldn't some women scream like that on finding the body of a friend?"

"She let loose like a maid in a TV murder mystery. You know, the ones who open a door, see a body, and drop a breakfast tray."

"How about Jack and Angie Palmer? Do you know anything about Jack's condition?"

"I only learned today. I hadn't seen Jack for a year and a half. He seemed a bit absentminded professorish then, but nothing shocking. He's must be going downhill fast." I rested my forearms on the table. "I can't see him bludgeoning someone and then pretending to be dazed and innocent. With his dementia, he lacks the conniving required to pull that off. Not to mention he's always been a kind man."

"And Angie Palmer?"

"If she caught Deborah in the act of stealing, she'd be furious, but she already knew one or more of her friends was stealing from her and killing her plants. Her plan was to expose them and run them out of the society, and that's why she invited me. What I can't figure out is why Deborah was on the stairs. She was near the top, wasn't she? You found blood high on the banister."

"It's preliminary, but I'd say she was hit at the top of the stairs or a step or two down. That information doesn't leave this house."

"So even a shorter woman, like Annabel, could have hit her on top of her head."

Rancourt pushed himself to a standing position and dragged his phone from his suit pocket. Suddenly I wished I'd fixed him coffee. He looked worn down, his energy depleted, the skin beneath his eyes dark. For Rancourt, the condition wasn't too appalling, but neither was it good.

"Do you have insomnia?" I asked.

He glanced up from his phone. "Sometimes."

"Me too. It helps to turn the lights low and get away from phones, TVs, and the rest for a couple hours before you go to bed." Thinking I'd probably overstepped my bounds, I fell silent and moved for the door. Rancourt was a private man, and personal advice didn't go down well with him. Though he *had* appreciated my gift of gummy-bear vitamins a few months back.

"Thanks," he said, trailing me. "I'll remember that. It's not doable when I'm working a case, though."

"I'll let you know if any of the others stop by."

As he made his way to his car, he called, "You can tell your friend Emily I've gone and it's safe to come over."

"Can't put one over on you, Detective," I shouted.

Okay, so maybe he hadn't taken my advice about insomnia too badly, I thought. Not if he could joke like that, in such an I-know-you kind of way. He knew why Emily had phoned and that I'd tell her everything the second he drove off. Everything except for him thinking Deborah was hit at the top of the stairs or a step or two down, that is. I'd agreed to keep mum on that. I shut the door and headed back to the kitchen to tell Minette she could climb out of her teacup.

She was already out of the cup and sitting on the hutch shelf, dangling her legs as though she were poolside and swinging them over the surface of the water.

"Kate, Kate. Listen to me."

"I'm listening." I dropped back to my chair and gazed down at Annabel's full coffee cup.

"Annabel is a liar."

My eyes shot to the hutch. "About what?"

"A lot of things. She has a lying way in her voice."

The doorbell rang again, and I told Minette to hold that thought while I let Emily in.

"Rancourt says hello," I said, ushering my friend inside.

She wiped her feet on the mat and strode for the kitchen. "Does he still look like he needs a long vacation?"

"He does. Have a seat. Minette says Annabel is a liar." Fairies, I'd learned, could sense fear, mendacity, love, anger, and other failings and emotions in the human voice. Minette was like a living lie detector. Only I'd known her to be wrong—or somewhat off—on occasion. That is, she wasn't always spot-on right. Still, she could confirm my instincts and, at times, sense what I couldn't.

Emily was all ears. She waved Minette down from the hutch. "What's Annabel lying about?"

"Many things because she's a liar." Minette took flight, her ivory and blush-pink wings beating just three times before she descended to the middle of the table. "She didn't like Deborah." For emphasis, she paused and shook her head slowly from side to side. "*At all*. She doesn't like Angie either. Annabel feels cheated. They all cheat her—that's what she thinks."

"Because of the Ivy Cottage business?"

"Yes, but maybe because of other things too. I couldn't tell. She was also worried about the detective, and she didn't believe what you said about mice."

Emily gave me a questioning look and I told her I'd explain later.

"I need to hear other voices," Minette said. "We need to investigate."

"Count me in," Emily said with a grin. "Let's meet here tonight. I have a lot of catching up to do on this case."

"Is Laurence okay with that?" I asked. "I'm beginning to realize we usually meet at my house, not yours. Does he, you know . . ."

"Object to me coming over here when we have a case in the works? Nope. He grabs a book from his stack, plants himself in his armchair, and reads away. He's in heaven. My husband needs lots of space, though he's sweet enough not to say so to my face. When he's not on the road, he cherishes his down time, and it wouldn't be down time with the two of us chattering away. Besides, we couldn't take Minette to my house, could we? Unless we tell Laurence about her."

"No!" Minette screamed.

Emily reared back in her chair.

"Minette's feeling a little fragile these days," I said. "You know—the evil fairies in the forest, Surette, and all."

Emily leaned forward and stuck out a finger, and Minette wrapped her arms around it. "I don't blame you, little one. The three of us will solve this murder, and then we'll take care of this Hacquetia beast once and for all."

Minette laid her head on Emily's finger, her short hair's gentle waves falling about her face. "Yes, Emily. Thank you. You are my friend."

Lately I'd been a little jealous of Emily's relationship with Minette, and as I watched Minette hug Emily's finger, seemingly with no intention of letting go, that jealously grew. I'd said roughly the same thing to Minette—that we'd rid the forest of Hacquetia—but I'd been met with doubt, not a hug. And *I'd* been the one to take Minette to the forest, hadn't I? The one the Green Blur of Evil had dive-bombed? For all I knew, that fairy could have been trying to poke my eyes out.

But rather than hug me, Minette enjoyed telling me I was angry. *Why are you so angry, Kate? Is it because Michael died?* Of course it was. I was as angry over what he'd suffered as Minette was over Hacquetia and her crew, and I would not make peace with the world.

"Okay, guys, let's stop hugging and get down to business, shall we?"

Emily withdrew her finger, but not before looking at me as though I were the crabby old lady on the block. The truth? I was only two years older than my next-door neighbor, but I may as well have been ten years her senior. Losing the love of your life can age you faster than anything. Emily, happily married to the still-living love of *her* life, had no idea. Then again, I *could* be a crab sometimes, and although I knew that about myself, I didn't care to correct the flaw.

"We need to come up with a plan," I said. "How do we get more information on these women and how can we get Minette within earshot of them while keeping her safe?"

Emily rose. "I'll think about it over dinner. And I'll ask Laurence if he knows any of the suspects."

I heard a ring and answered my phone without looking at the number. It was Angie. Jack was losing it, she said, and while fretting and talking nonstop, he'd said my name twice and asked to see me. He'd remembered me from the past, and he'd remembered seeing me standing near Deborah's body after he'd found the bloody ornament. Angie's hired nurse wouldn't be there for another hour and a half. Could I come over?

CHAPTER 7

I rang Angie's doorbell, thinking as I waited for her to answer how strange it was that Jack had remembered my name and remembered seeing me. I hadn't said a word to him after he'd brandished the bloody pineapple, yet he'd recognized me. "Stay quiet," I whispered. Minette had stowed away in my jeans pocket and was partially shielded by my long shirt, but I was well aware that she liked to take risks and would probably flee the safety of my pocket to do some exploring.

"Kate, thank you for coming," Angie said, practically pulling me inside. "Come, come. A minute ago he again asked to see you." She pushed the door shut behind me. "I don't know what he wants, but I think just seeing you will calm him. He likes familiar faces. Maybe when he saw you, it stirred memories from the past. Come with me."

I followed her through her front room and into her library, where Jack was sitting in a high-backed green leather armchair of the type you sometimes saw in very old and elegant public libraries. Angie invited me to sit on the chair next to his, with only a small, round table between us, though the nearest chair for her was on the other side of the room.

"Jack, hello," I said, taking my seat. "It's Kate Brewer."

Angie remained standing. "You asked to see Kate."

For a moment I thought he knew me, and then confusion, like a gray cloud scudding by, passed over his face. "Did I?"

Angie sighed. "It comes and goes like the wind."

"Jack." I angled myself to face him more directly. "Did you want to talk to me about the murder? Or maybe about the pineapple ornament you found?"

"Murder," he said, nodding slowly. "I'm very glad you're here. I remember you! There was a murder in this house."

I felt Minette start to wiggle her way out of my pocket. "That's right. And you found a pineapple ornament. Where did you find it?"

He pointed a bony finger my way. "That pineapple was in the wrong place. It was in my room."

Angie walked to the chair on the other side of the library and sat.

"Where did you find it in your room?" I asked.

"It didn't belong there," he said. "It belongs here, in the library. Look at all of them." He waved a hand. "You'd think they hatch in here."

I smiled. "They're pretty. But that one in your room didn't belong there."

"That's right. You've got it."

"Do you know how it got there?"

"Someone must have brought it. I have my suspicions."

"Who?"

He lifted a shoulder. "You got me. I'm just saying it didn't belong, and it's a strange matter."

"I agree. Do you know how blood got on it?"

"Blood? There's no blood."

"When you found it, there was blood on it."

Jack's eyes grew wide. "Does it have to do with the murder?"

"Well . . ." I looked to Angie, waiting for her permission to proceed. I didn't want to rile Jack and then leave it to her and his nurse to calm him down.

"Jack, dear," she said, "it *does* have to do with the murder. Someone hit Deborah Wetherbee on the head with it. Do you remember Deborah?"

"I don't remember anyone named Deborah."

"She's a friend," Angie said.

"I don't like those friends of yours. They creep around this house like cats."

"What do you mean?" Angie asked.

"They're like those butterflies I keep finding. Always out of place. I shoo them away."

Angie looked bewildered. "You shoo my friends? I don't understand."

"When they show up where they don't belong, my darling, I do." Jack looked about the library, his eyes moving from bookcase to bookcase, then across the ceiling and down to the rolling stairs at one end of the room. "I remember this place. I love books. I love the smell of them."

I leaned toward him, waiting to catch his attention before I spoke. "Jack, have you ever seen anything odd happen in this library or house? Or in the garden? Anything unusual involving one of the friends who creep around like cats?"

He winked. "Things have disappeared, you know. Here one minute, gone the next." He lowered his voice. "I've seen things going on in the garden. Teacups don't get up and walk away. They don't have legs, do they?" His eyes found Angie across the room. "Can I take a rest now?"

Poor Jack. He was further gone than I'd imagined. If this conversation was anything to go by, his lucid moments lasted about five seconds.

"Of course you can, dear. Are you hungry?"

"No, I'm tired. Too much is going on today. I've had enough of butterflies and beds and pills. Too many pills. And jam jars, all over the place. Jam jars."

I smiled a little on hearing his *jam jaahhs*. Jack's accent was as Downeast as Angie's. "Jam jars?" I asked.

"Don't tell me I'm imagining things," Jack said, pushing himself out of his chair. "I'm not a fool."

Fortunately for the two of them, Jack seemed steady on his feet. At least he hadn't lost mobility.

"I'll be back in a few minutes," Angie said, wrapping an arm around Jack's waist. "Take another look around the garden if you want, or fix yourself some tea in the kitchen."

Angie accompanied Jack upstairs, and I walked into the kitchen and out the French doors. A swarm of blue butterflies fluttering above tall purple delphiniums greeted me to my right, a few feet from the doors. No wonder the things got inside the kitchen. I smiled, thinking how pleased Annabel would be to know that some of her blue inmates had escaped their greenhouse prison.

"Out, out," Minette said quietly. "It's hot. Your pocket is tight."

"You've told me that before."

She climbed halfway up my shirt and then, pushing off with her legs, barreled into the clear blue sky. Loose in a colorful garden, she was less likely to be spotted, I reasoned, so I let her fly. Anyway, I'd left the window to my Jeep open, so she could always hide there. But I'd noticed lately that she'd become unusually careless around other humans. She didn't understand, or didn't want to know, the danger she'd be in if anyone laid eyes on her. She'd end up in a net or jar, and that thought filled me with horror.

As I waited for Angie to return, I went over the events leading up the discovery of Deborah's body. Maybe I'd missed a clue hidden within the seemingly mundane conversation and behavior of Angie's friends. Harry appeared to be a mild-mannered guy, a flower-loving man among women who didn't mind his only-man status much. Angie had told me he'd been the first male to run the society, his term ending eight months ago when Angie was elected head of their group.

I had considered Annabel the open, candid type, but I'd since revised that opinion. She was hiding something. Yet as silly as her concern for Angie's butterflies was in view of how harsh nature could be, I rather liked that she felt sympathy for them. And Maya? She was a tough cookie, declaring shamelessly that I wasn't at the tea party to have tea and talk gardening. That was true, of course, but to keep pressing the point? *Rude.*

In a similar way, Deborah had been a little rough around the edges, and just maybe she'd enjoyed rubbing salt in Annabel's Ivy Cottage wounds. *Are you trying to bring someone else into the company?* She'd known how much Annabel was hoping to join the company, but she'd deliberately tweaked her.

When one of the butterflies headed for the open French doors, I closed them behind me. Running my hand over the delphiniums, more butterflies scattered. And then something caught my eye.

Parting the crowded stems, I saw a small book resting on its spine at the base of the plants. I reached in, pulled it out, and brushed soil from the cover. *The Maine Flower Garden* looked to be an older volume, perhaps rare. Its pages were puckered, damaged by rain or sprinkler water by the looks of it. Was it one of Angie's missing books, presumed stolen?

Looking back toward the French doors I saw Angie approach and I held up the book. She pushed through the doors, a frown creasing her face.

"It was in the delphiniums." I pointed to where I'd found it. "Is this one of your stolen books?"

"I know with absolute certainty it is." She snatched the book from my hands. "I'd planned to give this to a charity auction in May but I couldn't find it. Look at the state of it, Kate. It's ruined."

"Water damage."

Angie ran her fingers over the wrinkled title page then gave me an exasperated look. "Well, for crying out loud, who put it there? Who would do such a destructive thing? I can understand theft, but this? You know criminals. Tell me what someone was thinking. What's the point of this destruction?"

"I don't know, Angie, and I sure don't know criminal minds. They're a mystery to me. Is someone trying to get back at you for something?" I shrugged, indicating I was only taking a wild guess.

"That must be it. And you know, it does just that. It galls me. This book would have raised five hundred dollars for charity—and preserved the book."

"Good heavens."

"A so-called friend . . ."

"Could it have been an accident?" I was clutching at straws, but I hated to think that one of Angie's friends had destroyed the precious volume on purpose, and more than that, I hated that Angie suspected her friends of being cruel.

"Yes, Kate, someone took it out of the library, dropped it smack in the middle of my delphiniums, and forgot to pick it up."

"I know it's unlikely, but—"

"No, this was a deliberate act." She clutched the book to her chest and gazed out over her garden. "Could the other books be here? Are they ruined too? I'd rather think of them as stolen and hidden away in someone else's library than dumped like trash."

"Let's find out."

"We can't search the whole garden."

"No, but let's start with the area near the doors and then move in the direction of the greenhouse. Have you dead-headed your roses in the past week or so?"

"All those tasks have slipped my mind. I'm terribly behind my schedule."

"Then we should check the roses too." On my left was another island of purple delphiniums, and beyond them, some variety of yellow daylily, still blooming profusely. I began my search with the delphiniums, parting stems and training my eyes on the ground, and then I moved to the daylilies.

"That's my 'Bess Ross' daylily," Angie said proudly. "Last year it slowed down by mid-July, but this year it shows no signs of letting up."

A hint of white glinted among the lilies' slender leaves. "What's this?"

Angie came alongside me as I bent low, retrieved a teacup, and put it in her hands.

"My eighth cup," she said, her voice turned faint with disbelief. "I assumed one of the society members had broken it and was afraid to tell me."

Continuing my search, I soon found the matching saucer. "It doesn't look damaged," I said, turning it over in my hands. "The cup?"

"It looks all right."

"No cracks or chips?"

"No."

"Good. I wonder what else we'll find. It's like a treasure hunt, isn't it?"

Angie had gone silent. I tried to cheer her by pointing out that at least she had her beautiful porcelain cup back, but she would have none of it. "I've always considered them my *friends*. I won't be able to look at them anymore, knowing that one of them did this—or *more* than one of them, Kate! Does this seem like the work of one person? I don't think so."

I thought a moment. And then I decided to fudge the truth a bit. I'd found two stolen items within a few steps of her French doors. How many others were out there, spread across her two acres? It was possible that stealing and dumping her belongings required a team effort. And if only one of Angie's friends was doing the actual stealing, were her other friends complicit in their silence? Had they seen what was happening and stayed silent? Or approved of it? "Sure, it could be one person, Angie, and it's possible we won't find anything else in your garden."

"In the garden or not, there's still the matter of the thefts. Let me put this teacup in my kitchen before I drop it."

She took the saucer from my hand and headed back to the house.

As I circled around, deciding where to go next, I had a thought. Veering right, I walked until I was right below Jack's second-floor window. Then, moving in a more or less straight line, I walked backward, stepping away from the house until I felt I was in a location where Jack could see me clearly if he came to his window. Behind me, an island of mixed flowers bloomed: whites, blues, and buttercream yellows.

I started combing through the stems and leaves, and thirty seconds into my hunt, I found a half-full jar of orange marmalade. Was this one of the jam jars Jack had said were all over the place? Maybe he wasn't so far gone after all. *I've seen things going on in the garden. Teacups don't get up and walk away.*

Minette rocketed in from somewhere behind me, landed in my hair, and clawed her way like a giant bug to the back of my neck. "I almost swatted you," I hissed.

She yanked on my hair. "Look up, Kate! See the window!"

I gazed up at the house.

Jack waved at me. He'd been watching me from his bedroom window.

"Jam jars and teacups," I said under my breath. What else had Jack seen from that window?

CHAPTER 8

Although Jack had trouble expressing himself and was confused much of the time, it was apparent he sometimes saw exactly what he said he saw, as evidenced by the teacup and marmalade jar in the garden. I needed to reassess everything he'd said to me, and so did Angie.

I told Minette to tuck herself back in my jeans pocket and then brought the marmalade jar to Angie. She was in the kitchen, talking with a woman I assumed was Jack's nurse, so I didn't elaborate after telling her I'd found the jar in a flower bed. Angie said nothing, but her pained expression was eloquence itself.

"I'm Kate Brewer," I said, introducing myself to the nurse. "A friend of the family."

"Mary Davidson, Jack Palmer's nurse," the woman said as she continued to unpack her canvas bag. She set her items on the counter, then looked them over: a small bottle of some kind of energy drink, a couple sandwiches in plastic wrap, a newly filled prescription in a paper bag, two cans of Coke. "Nice to meet you. Let me put these in the fridge." She grabbed the sandwiches and Cokes and laid them on a shelf in Angie's stainless refrigerator.

"Jack and I just talked," I said.

"Oh?" Mary folded her canvas bag into quarters, pushed her glasses to the bridge of her nose, and gave me her full attention. She was young, crisp of manner, and efficient.

"I hadn't seen him in well over a year."

"Oh, yes? I've been here—what is it, Angie?—about six months. It's nice to meet another of Jack's friends. He's a kind man."

"I don't know if you heard, but there was an incident here earlier today." Someone had to broach the subject. Anyway, I wanted to pick Mary's brains about Jack.

Looking rather dejected, Angie leaned against the counter. "Kate is being polite. One of my garden society friends was murdered in the front room."

Mary sucked in her breath and let her hands dangle at her sides. "No. Seriously? Oh, Angie, that's terrible! What happened?"

I let Angie carry on with the details. Besides not wanting to bring up Jack and the bloody ornament unless Angie approved, I could feel Minette stirring in my pocket and knew from experience she was about to take off. I strode for the library, telling Angie I needed to check her books and I'd be right back.

The instant I crossed the threshold into the library, Minette shot out of my pocket, dove for one of the bookcases, slowed to a flutter, and then came to a rest on top of a large volume. "Kate, Kate!"

"*Shhh.*" I put a finger to my lips and glanced behind me to make sure we were alone.

"Jack was telling the truth," she said. "He's not a liar."

"That's what I think too."

"Now I must see his room. *Now.*"

"You can't let him see you."

Minette gave me one of her honey-butter smiles. "It's safe. No one would believe him if he said he saw me. They wouldn't believe you, either."

I shook my head. "Promise me you won't let him see you. If he does, he'll tell Angie, and that would upset her terribly."

"I promise, Kate. I can hide very well."

"But you're getting careless, and you don't understand how dangerous that is."

"Careful, careful. I'll be more careful than I am in the Smithwell Forest, and I'm very careful there."

Reluctantly, I let her go. With fears of Hacquetia foremost in her mind, respite in the form of an investigation was going do her good. Aside from that, her senses were sharp, especially her hearing, and though she often didn't grasp the full significance of what she was seeing, her powers of observation were exceptional.

Was she a little like Jack in that respect? Seeing clearly but not fully understanding? I cringed at the comparison. Poor Jack. I regretted not spending more time with him. How many more days did he have at home before Angie would be forced to leave him in full-time care?

I scanned the bookshelves, marveling at the old gardening and botanical books, even recognizing some of the authors' names: Frederick Law Olmsted, William Kent, Gertrude Jekyll. Many of the volumes looked to be first editions. Angie's library was a treasure chest. Still, for her, the stolen books weren't primarily a financial loss; they signified a broken friendship.

"Can you believe this library?"

The voice broke into my thoughts. I pivoted back as Mary ambled her way across the room.

"Do you get a chance to read any of them?" I asked.

"I love the gardening books you're looking at. Those old ones. So does Jack, though he can't remember why. I sometimes take him a book, if he's in the mood, and I either let him page through it or I read it to him. When he falls asleep, I sometimes stay beside his bed and read a while to make sure he's really asleep. So in that sense I do get a chance, yes. By the way, Angie said to tell you she's upstairs and she'll be down in a minute."

Angie hadn't run screaming from the second floor, so I figured Minette had hidden herself in time. "Thanks. Are you saying Jack remembers liking gardening, but he can't recall why?"

"That's about it. His tastes are much the same as they ever were, but the memories connected to those tastes are missing."

"What do you mean you read a while to make sure he's really asleep?"

"He can wake up startled sometimes, until he falls into a deeper sleep."

I slid Gertrude Jekyll's *Gardens for Small Country Houses* from the shelf. "Can I ask you something about him?"

"I thought that's what you were doing."

"Sorry. I'm trying to help Angie figure out who's been stealing her things. Books, library ornaments, teacups." Certain there were more thieves at work than Annabel, I didn't mention her confession about the pineapple ornaments.

"She hasn't said anything to me about that. How many things? Since when?"

"Someone's been stealing for months." To reassure her that she wasn't under suspicion, I added, "Angie's narrowed it down to one or more of her garden society friends."

Curiously, Mary didn't look surprised. "And you're wondering if I've seen anything suspicious?"

"Or if Jack has and he's said anything to you. He's very observant."

"He can be."

"There was a pineapple ornament from the library in his bedroom. He said it was out of place."

"Oh, that." She smiled. "He asked for it. Sometimes when I bring him a book, he'll tell me how much he misses the library and how he'd rather sleep there than his bedroom. He likes the smell and feel of the books, the look of the lamps, the pictures on the wall, the ornaments." She leaned in, and with a sad lilt to her voice said, "Once in a while he asks me for what he calls 'memories' of the library. The library he's not sure is his. Last time he wanted one of those pineapple ornaments, and since there are so many here, I brought him one and left it in his room. It gave him pleasure for a while."

"Did Angie know you did that?"

She squinted at me through her black-rimmed glasses. Now I was offending her professionalism. "I don't tell her every little thing I do. How would that be any relief to her? When I take over, Angie Palmer relaxes."

"And I'm so glad you're here to give her a break. I'm only gathering as much information as I can. The thing is, Angie *hired* me to investigate, and I can't let her down." Now I was emphasizing my own professionalism, as well as telling her that remuneration was involved, meaning I was obliged to ask insensitive questions.

Mary relaxed. "I see. Well, now, with that library ornament? Two of Angie's gardening friends saw me take it from a shelf. They were in here, arguing over who knows what, and when I walked in, they hushed. I said hello, took the ornament, and left. They can't vouch that I didn't steal it, but they can tell you I was open about what I was doing."

"Who were they?"

"Harry and Maya. They were standing about where you are now."

"Did you catch any of their argument?"

Mary closed her eyes for a moment, trying to remember. "Maya said something like 'We can't make money from that,' and Harry said something like 'I know what people buy,' and then something about how he knows marketing. Then I walked in and they hushed up."

The clip of Angie's heels on oak floors signaled her arrival. "Hushed up? Who hushed up?"

I jumped in. "I'm afraid I've been bothering Mary with questions regarding my investigation."

Angie nodded. "Good call. Mary's very observant. So who hushed up?"

"Maya and Harry," Mary said. "A few days ago I came into the library for one of the pineapple ornaments, and they seemed to be arguing. Then went quiet when they saw me."

Angie frowned. "One of the ornaments? What on earth for?"

"For Jack." Mary proceeded to explain that she often brought things to Jack's bedroom to comfort or quiet him. "Eventually, they all go back where they belong. I hope that's all right."

"It's a good idea," Angie said thoughtfully. "Of course it's all right. I've noticed that different objects or sounds soothe him at different times."

"Well, that explains why the ornament was in his room," I said.

"Yes, yes." A faraway look came into Angie's eyes. "The other ornaments and books aren't in Jack's room, though. And he wouldn't hide them, would he, Mary?"

Mary was vehement in her response. "No way, Angie. It wouldn't enter his mind, and in any case he's not capable. If he hid something for who knows what reason, the very next minute he'd be telling you where it is."

It was time for me to go, for Mary to take over and leave Angie to her rest. I tapped the Jekyll volume I was still holding. "Isn't this the book Harry wanted to borrow? If you give me his address? I'll take it to him."

"If you're sure you want to go to the trouble." She shot me a quizzical look, probably thinking, and quite rightly, that I was up to something sneaky. "Let me get his address for you."

The moment Angie exited the library, Mary pulled a small notepad and miniature pen from her pants pocket. She scribbled something, tore a sheet from the notepad, and stuffed the paper in my hand. "Call me tomorrow morning," she whispered, "and don't say a word to Angie."

CHAPTER 9

H arry Jelinek was watering flowerpots on his porch when I drove up to his white cottage-style house on the far east side of Smithwell. Hearing the grind of my tires on gravel, he turned, set down his watering can, and headed down the porch steps, meeting me at the top of his driveway. Naturally I assumed he intercepted me to avoid inviting me into his home, but when he took the book, he asked me inside for a cup of decaf coffee. The thought of coffee on an empty stomach was unpleasant, but I accepted in order to gain entry to his house.

Telling me his wife was pruning in the back garden, he led me to a small dining room off his kitchen. Minette was already squirming in my right pocket. If she was going to hitch a ride with me, we'd have to come up with a better plan, I thought. I worried every time I sat that I was smothering her in my denim.

"The mosquitoes don't bother her this time of evening?" I asked.

"She's immune. It's me they go for." He pushed aside a short stack of large picture frames, a yellow legal notepad, and some rough drawings that might have been Ivy Cottage ad copy to make room for us at the table. Then he started the coffee maker. "Thanks for driving out here. Have a seat. Pound cake?"

Food, thank goodness. "I'd love some." I sat with caution, leaning a little to my left to give Minette more room.

"Have you ever read Gertrude Jekyll?"

"No, but I've always wanted to. This book looks good."

He set a plate of sliced pound cake, two smaller plates, and a couple forks on the table, then sat. "But you didn't drive out here just to bring me the book."

I forced a smile and gave myself time to think of a response by transferring a slice of pound cake to my plate.

"My wife says I leap to the point too quickly," he said. "Sorry about that. I go from A to Z, no stops in between, no nice preliminaries."

"It's called being straightforward, and I appreciate it."

"Then I'm right? The book was an excuse? Not that I don't appreciate the effort."

"Can I ask you some questions?" I took a bite of cake.

"You're still helping Angie?"

I swallowed. "What do you know about that?"

"Only what Maya suspected." He rose, poured two cups of coffee, and retook his seat. "Decaf, no jitters," he said, sliding a cup my way. "She said you're a crime investigator, so ipso facto, you were at Angie's house to solve a crime. She told me not to talk to you."

"I don't remember her telling you not to talk to me."

He took a long, slow drink of coffee. "This was as we were leaving Angie's. Maya is a suspicious woman."

"Why is she suspicious of me?"

"You mean why is she suspicious if she has nothing to hide? That's the question."

The coffee looked and smelled like tar, but wanting to appear cordial and buy more time, I took a sip. "Well, even people who have nothing to hide might not want to be questioned by a stranger, but she was awfully contentious from the get-go."

"That's Maya too. She's a boxer. Offense is her best defense."
He took another slow sip of his coffee, watching me over the rim
of his cup. Ours was a conversation of long pauses, both of us
trying to goad the other into saying something to fill the in-be-
tween moments. From experience I knew such slip-ups—things
said to soothe the silences—sometimes produced incriminating
evidence.

I changed my approach. "How long have you known Angie
and the others?"

"I've known Angie more than six years. Her first, then the
others through the Smithwell Garden Society."

"You were the first male president."

"I was glad to let Angie take the reins. It's a lot of phone
and paperwork. Loads of organizing and fund-raising, and that
leaves less time for gardening." Another long sip. "So Kate,
here's what I'm thinking. There's a reason you came to our
meeting rather than visit Angie on her own. What crime are
you working on?"

It was going to come out anyway, so I answered honestly. In
part. "Angie thinks some of her plants have been poisoned with
an herbicide."

"That's bananas. How could that happen? She doesn't use
herbicides."

This was a man who had trouble grasping what was in front
of his face. "No, she thinks someone brought the herbicide in.
A number of her plants died overnight."

Harry's mouth tightened. "And she thinks one of us did it? I
think I'm getting your point now."

"The poisonings happened when the society gathered at her
house."

"What kind of herbicide was used? Organic or synthetic?"

"Angie hasn't had the dead plants tested. Is anyone envious of her garden?"

"We all are! You said the plants died overnight?"

"That's right. In twelve hours or less."

"That sounds like a synthetic herbicide. Organic herbicides don't often work that fast." As he took another drink of coffee, I could see the spark of a new thought cross his face. He set his cup down. "But look, none of us would kill her plants, and we sure wouldn't use a synthetic herbicide to do it. We label our Ivy Cottage products 'natural.' Spraying synthetics in her garden would be cutting our own throats. There are regulations about what you can call natural or organic. Our reputation is at stake. Were any of the dead plants calendula or chamomile?"

"She said part of her chamomile field was ruined. A few square feet."

"I haven't looked at her garden in weeks, but that makes no sense. The chamomile—the *company's* chamomile—destroyed? Although . . ."

"What?"

"Maya accused Angie of using synthetic herbicides, pesticides, and fungicides in her garden. I thought it was just Maya being Maya, but what if there was something to her accusation?"

"When was this?"

"Something like three months ago."

"Why would Angie use her own money to bankroll the company and then take a risk like that?"

Harry shook his head emphatically. "She wouldn't. So why did Maya say that?"

And why are you carefully implicating Maya? I heard the scrape of a sliding glass door moving in its track somewhere beyond the dining room. "What would make her think Angie was using synthetics?"

"Earlier in the year, her calendula was being ravaged by aphids, and Maya thinks she used an insecticidal spray on them. Aphids gone in a day, sticky plants left behind."

I frowned. "That's not much evidence to go on, and aphids leave a sticky residue on their own."

"She also told me she saw a spray bottle under Angie's kitchen sink."

"She was snooping around under her sink? It might have been for indoor use."

"I doubt it."

"Janice," Harry said, rising to give his wife a hand. He took a potted geranium and pair of pruners from her, and without mentioning why we were talking, she introduced me as Angie's friend.

"Are you in the Smithwell Garden Society?" she asked, settling into a chair. She removed her dirt-soiled gloves and set them next to the picture frames. "Harry, this is too much. We need to clear this table."

"Soon as I'm done," he replied.

Janice grinned and rolled her eyes at me. *Husbands, eh?* She was a few years younger than Harry, maybe in her mid-forties, with thick blonde-gray hair and bright skin.

Deciding not to pass up the opportunity to hear what she thought about Annabel, Maya, and Angie, I threw caution to the wind—and ignored Harry, who was at the counter snipping a dead bloom from the geranium and casting a wary eye my way. "Did you hear about Deborah?"

"It's so awful," she said. "The police questioned everyone."

"I know, I was there."

"Was she really murdered?"

Harry let go of his geranium and sat next to Janice. "I was hoping to put it out of my mind for a while."

"Yes, she was murdered," I answered. "Angie is heartbroken. She can't think who hated her enough."

Janice's blue eyes narrowed. "It wasn't Harry, if you're implying that."

Harry may have been slow to fathom what was going on around him, but his wife had grasped my meaning in a heartbeat. "No, no. To tell you the truth, Angie wonders if it was Maya or Annabel."

Harry was astonished. "Does she? Jack's the one who was holding the bloody ornament."

"Jack wouldn't hurt a fly," Janice said. "Maya's the nasty one. Hard as nails, that woman."

"Annabel seemed to resent being left out of Ivy Cottage."

"She did," Janice said, letting her shoulders relax as she reclined in her chair. "She still does. She wanted in, and she complained to Harry about not being part of the company. But it's so *small* right now. They can't absorb more people without risking collapse."

Harry nodded his agreement. "We couldn't afford her, and that's that."

"You said earlier you have plans to hire three employees soon. Did you offer Annabel a position?"

"Sure, but she didn't want one," Harry said. "She was insulted when I asked her if she'd like a job when we launched the hand lotion. She was angry with me, believe it or not. Angry at being given a job—imagine."

"So she turned down the job offer?"

"I confess it didn't pay well," Harry replied. "I wouldn't have taken it either."

Janice grabbed her gloves and stood. "I don't know these women as well as Harry does, but if someone at that meeting killed Deborah—"

"It *was* someone in the house," I said. "No doubt about it."

"Then my money is on Maya Estabrook."

"You ought to talk to her," Harry said. He held up a finger. "I know just the excuse you need. I was going to lend her one of *my* garden books. You can tell her you stopped by my house to give me the Jekyll, and in return, I gave you my book on Italian gardens to take to her. She lives in an apartment downtown."

Another book errand made me the society's courier, but I needed an excuse to question Maya, and taking her the book was as good a scheme as any I could come up with on the spur of the moment. "What do *you* think about Maya, Harry? Does she have the capacity to commit murder?"

"She has the heart. She's the only one of us who has the heart to murder."

I got to my feet.

"Before you go, would you like to see our back garden?" Janice asked. "It's coming along nicely."

"We don't want to bore her," Harry said.

"Oh, come on, Harry," I said. "I want to see this master plan you're working on. Maybe I can pick up a few tips for my own garden."

Janice laughed as she walked ahead of me to the sliding glass door and led me out to her garden. "I don't know about a master plan," she said, gazing out over her yard. "I think gardens are years if not decades in the making. But I think we've made strides the past two years."

Their sizable back yard was surrounded by a newish looking cedar fence, its golden color not yet grayed out by rain and sun. Four young trees sat at each corner of the yard, and work had begun digging out two kidney-shaped flower beds toward the back. Near the patio where we stood was a small rose garden, and drifting through it like a river, a swath of white petunias making one last summer show.

Unreasonably, their unfinished and quite ordinary garden made me feel better about my own front and back yards. I'd told the truth when I'd said my garden-design method was to find plants I like and dig holes for them. And yet, looking out over Harry and Janice's garden and considering its overall appearance, my method hadn't served me poorly.

"Master plan," Janice said with a giggle. "Like most people, we're playing it by ear."

I glanced back into the house, where Harry was now standing with what I presumed was the book I was to take to Maya. "Harry said he's studying the greats of garden design, to get the structure right."

"Is he now?" Janice made a face. "Then how come I'm doing most of the work?"

CHAPTER 10

Maya's apartment building was at the crest of a small hill, and the red brick buildings of Smithwell's small downtown sat clustered beneath it. "You have a beautiful view," I said, admiring the picture-postcard scene out her living room window. A few blocks off was the towering white steeple of the area's oldest church. Both imposing and cheering, it was my favorite building in all of Smithwell as well as a signpost marking the northern end of the downtown area.

"I'd rather have my house back, but yeah, it's not bad. It's prettiest at night." She handed me the glass of water I'd asked for. "My gardening is limited to some pots on my bedroom balcony, and that's not really a balcony. It's a blip. You couldn't fit people on it. But after my divorce"—she spread her arms out, presenting the small living room and even smaller open kitchen behind it—"this is what I ended up with. Seven hundred square feet. Promise me you won't say it's cozy."

"Not a word. But I *do* like your view. Honestly. Do you live alone?"

"Yup. You?"

"In my house? Yes. My husband died more than a year and a half ago."

"Sorry." As she sank into the lone couch in the room, she fastened her eyes on me. "Do you think we can be honest with each other? Maybe, possibly?"

"I hope so."

"Take a load off and let's give it a shot." She extended her hand toward a low-back stuffed chair in the corner, and though I wanted to remain standing for poor Minette's sake, I complied.

"What are we going to be honest about?" I asked, a touch of sarcasm in my voice. Maya rubbed me the wrong way. I disliked people who considered rudeness a virtue.

"You're here to question me about Deborah's death. You think I did it. Harry told me."

"When was this?"

"Just now. He phoned to say you were on your way and your excuse to pester me was that book you brought. You think I'm a murderer."

"Funny, but Harry's the one who suggested I bring the book."

To my shock, she let loose with a loud laugh and slapped her hands together. "He's a weasel, that man! Playing both sides, throwing chum in the water. I should have known."

"What do you mean?"

"Don't you see?" With some effort Maya managed to stop laughing. "He suggested you question me, subtly I'm sure, but then he phoned me, pretending to come to my defense. He didn't think I'd tell you because he doesn't think that far ahead. He's not a planner. Makes me wonder if he killed Deborah—that didn't look planned. I wouldn't have thought so, but he *is* a supreme weasel. I'll bet he led you to believe I had a motive for killing Deborah. Am I right? Come on, what did he say?"

Briefly, I pondered if I should divulge the details of my private conversation with Harry. But realizing that Harry *was* a weasel for phoning Maya behind my back, I concluded I owed him nothing. "Harry thinks you killed Deborah. He said you're the only one with the heart to do it. He also hinted that you might have something to do with the synthetic herbicide that killed some of Angie's plants."

This time Maya's mouth dropped, her lips forming an O shape as though she were about to blow a smoke ring. I couldn't get past how round her face was, and her rounded lips and bob hairdo made it more so.

"Wha—what?" she sputtered. "What proof does he have? Tell me what he said."

It was a strange answer. When confronted with such an accusation, most innocent people would first have proclaimed their innocence, not asked about the evidence. "He said you accused Angie of using synthetic herbicides, pesticides, and fungicides in her garden."

"So the accuser becomes the accused?" She lifted her wrist to check her watch. "It's seven-thirty."

"Time I left?"

"No." She stood abruptly. "We have half an hour before they close. Come with me."

When Maya led me down a flight of stairs and out the front door of her building, I realized we were headed somewhere downtown. I didn't ask where. I just followed, intrigued by the shift in her anger. I was no longer the target. Harry was.

She walked with determination, and I half-raced to keep up with her. I felt Minette rise above the hem of my jeans pocket but let her be. Anyone who saw me would guess I had a child's toy in my pocket. It had happened before, in fact. People saw what they wanted to see.

Three blocks later we were at Brentwood and Bowers, an antiques shop on Essex Street. The shop was empty except for an employee behind the sales counter, a young man who brightened considerably at the sight of two customers. "Hello, I'm Anthony. May I help you ladies?"

"I'll let you know," Maya said. She moved for the back of the long, narrow shop, coming to a stop in front of a wall of framed prints and engravings. Scowling and propping her hands on her hips, she nodded at the wall, as if to say, *That settles it.*

"What am I looking at?" I asked.

"Take a closer look."

"They're old prints," I said, stating the obvious. "Views of gardens, botanicals. They look original—and judging by the wrinkles, some of them are on thin paper. The others aren't. The frames aren't as old, so they're not original."

She turned to me with a triumphant smirk on her face. "Harry sold maybe ten of these on this wall. I caught him two weeks ago. At first I thought he was buying, but he was selling. I was here trying to sell some of my ex-husband's antique nautical stuff." She leaned sideways and whispered, "He doesn't even miss it."

One large print on fine paper bore a stunning price tag: four hundred dollars. The label next to the frame read, "Common daisy, hand-colored folio engraving from *Flora Londinensis* by William Curtis, 1798."

"That's from one of the volumes of Angie's *Flora Londinensis*," Maya said. "Old and very precious."

"Are you sure?"

"Positive. The book this print came from is still in her library, but other prints have been neatly razored out of it, and I know for a fact Harry borrowed the volume last month."

Maya's attitude astounded me. "You didn't tell Angie?"

"I meant to, but Harry—"

"Why did he borrow a book like that? It's full of botanical prints, not garden designs and advice."

"He told Angie that Janice, his wife, was learning to water-color and wanted to see it."

From the corner of my eye I saw the shop's lone employee approach us. Smiling and rubbing his hands together, he sensed a sale.

"Excuse me, but what can you tell me about this print?" I asked him.

His smile grew wider.

"It's an original hand-colored print from volume two of *Flora Londinensis*. Beautiful, isn't it? We have several other prints from the same first edition."

"Is it unusual to find prints that have been removed from a book?"

"Not at all. Sometimes the seller sees more of a profit from individual prints, especially if not all the engravings are in this nice of a condition. Other times, singular prints are all the seller has. They might have been passed down in the family. Nevertheless, the two-volume set of *Flora Londinensis* in good condition would bring at least twenty thousand dollars."

Maya presented me with another one of her I-told-you-so looks, and I grew angry. "Anthony, has Brentwood and Bowers ever received stolen engravings or prints?" By deliberately choosing the word *received*, I hope to shake him up and loosen his lips. Being fooled into purchasing stolen items was one thing, but it was quite another to be complicit in "receiving stolen goods," as the police termed it.

His spine went straight as a board. "We don't deal in anything stolen. We're a reputable establishment, more than a hundred years in this location."

"*This* may be stolen," I said, pointing at the daisy engraving.

"No, that's not possible. It came to us already framed, from an impeccable source. I *know* the man."

Then it hit me. I was taking Maya's word on the provenance of the engraving. What if it wasn't from Angie's book? And what if Harry had nothing to do with selling it? Or what if he'd legitimately purchased it himself and had resold it for a little cash? Maya clearly hated Harry—what wouldn't she do to harm him or his reputation? I would not blacken his name on so little evidence.

Still furious over Harry's betrayal, Maya had other ideas. "I know your source, and you're mistaken. He's sold you lots of botanical and garden prints, hasn't he?"

Anthony issued Maya a look of contempt and repeated his claim that the shop didn't deal with dodgy goods. "Would you like to leave now, please? I'm closing up."

"It's not eight o'clock yet," Maya snarled.

"It is for us," I said, grabbing Maya by the arm and hauling her out the shop's door. If Harry *had* sold the daisy engraving, his name was now mud. Antique shops kept thorough records, and Anthony would make the Harry connection without trouble. Not that I felt a lot of pity for the weasel, but to publicly declare someone a thief without proof positive was beyond the pale.

Out on the sidewalk, I turned on Maya. "If Angie's your friend and you're so sure Harry cut prints from her valuable book, why haven't you told her? You said nothing after he asked for the Gertrude Jekyll book at our tea."

Maya started to walk off, but I circled around her and blocked her path.

"I'm not real happy with Angie right now," she said.

I snorted. "Oh, that's a great reason. You're an accomplice now, do you get that? A priceless book was destroyed and you were a party to that. You should have told Detective Rancourt when he was at the house."

"It's got nothing to do with me!" she squawked, jabbing a thumb toward the antiques shop. "I'm not responsible, and if you tell the police what I said, I'll say you're making it up. Or I'll tell them I only put the pieces together while we were talking, just now, and we decided to come here for a look."

"Talk to Angie. Tell her your part in this before I do."

"It's your word against mine, Kate."

She was right about that. I stepped aside and let her go.

It was eight in the evening, and the sun was setting in the cloudless sky. Time for Minette and me to drive home. I headed for my Jeep, which I'd parked behind Maya's building, my empty stomach grumbling at me. At home, I would grab a quick bite, and then Emily and I would talk. Later, I'd find a way to tell Angie that Harry and Annabel had been stealing from her and Maya knew about it.

My way out of the parking lot was slowed by what passed for moderate traffic in downtown Smithwell: a line of five cars. Bringing up the rear was a white BMW, its driver a man with longish, graying hair. He turned my way as he drove by, shadows and the last orange rays of the sun playing over the driver's side glass.

A chill raced down my spine.

Ignace Surette. No doubt in my mind.

What was the man doing in Smithwell? He must have known the entire police force was after him. They knew his eccentric appearance, they knew he drove an ostentatious BMW in a town full of Ford and Chevy pickups. The gall of him to turn and smile at me! What game was he playing now?

"Kate, Kate."

"We're going." I pulled out of the lot and drove for Birch Street. Minette was on the floor of the front passenger side, and she grinned from ear to ear when I tilted the air-conditioning vent her way. Surette's name did not cross my lips. I didn't want to frighten her when I couldn't be certain he'd seen me.

Oh, but he had.

"Maya is a liar too," Minette said.

"You're right. And Harry?"

"He doesn't like the others. Those people don't like each other. Why do they eat together?"

"Good question. What about Mary Davidson, the nurse?"

"She has secrets to tell you, but she doesn't want to tell you now."

"I have to remember to call her in the morning. And what about Jack?"

"Jack likes everybody. But he has secrets too. When I was in the room, I heard him say things he didn't tell you."

"Who was he talking to?"

"To himself. He said, 'That cat, that sneaky cat. She comes here on the prowl. And *now* look look at the trouble she cause d.'"

CHAPTER 11

"**I** just ordered a large pizza, and you're welcome to have some," I told Emily as she settled into my couch. "I haven't eaten since tea at Angie's and I'm dying."

Minette had already eaten. Sitting cross-legged on my coffee table, stuffed with blueberries and contented as could be, she began to regale Emily with her keen sense of intuition. Annabel, Maya, Angie, and Harry—they were all liars in one sense or another, or at least they were holding something back, not telling the full truth. Mary Davidson also knew more than she'd been willing to say. "Even Jack lies," Minette said. "They all have secrets."

"Does Jack know he's lying?" Emily asked.

"Maybe he's afraid," I said. I stuck out my hand. "Give me that wine bottle." I debated telling her about seeing Surette and decided against it. Then I told myself I hadn't really seen him. He wasn't a stupid man and he wouldn't risk returning to Smithwell. I'd had him on my brain lately, that was all, and seeing him was a trick of my anxious mind. That had to be it.

Emily gave me the pinot and I smiled in anticipation. Pizza, wine, and desperate hunger—was there a finer combination?

"What is Mary Davidson lying about?" she asked.

"She's not lying exactly. Whatever she knows, she didn't want to say in front of Angie." I stopped peeling the wrap from the bottleneck and looked Emily square in the eye. "She didn't kill Deborah, I know that. She couldn't have because wasn't there. But what if she's stolen some of Angie's things and wants to confess?"

"If she wants to confess, she'll tell Angie, not you."

"Good point. Then again, she doesn't want to lose her job and I could act as a buffer between her and Angie." I was twisting the corkscrew into the bottle when I heard a knock. Pizza! I dashed for the front door as though I hadn't eaten in days and flung it open.

"Hello, Kate. You look like you were expecting someone else."

Harry. What was *he* doing here? "We just talked," I said, rudeness inching into my voice. "I'm about to eat, Harry, and I really need to eat."

"Mind if I come in for a moment?" he pleaded. He took one step over the threshold and rested his shoulder on the door jamb. "Five minutes of your time? I gave you *my* time."

He glanced at Emily as she walked past the door. My friend was letting him know I wasn't alone in the house. Unlike Angie, I'd had good luck in the friendship department.

"We should talk somewhere private, though," he added. "Five minutes, that's all."

"Two minutes. Emily and I are about to eat." I waved him back outside, much to his shock, and stood there, my arms folded across my chest, my expression stern. *Don't speak hogwash to me, Harry. Spill it.*

"We're going to talk out here?"

"This is as private as it gets. I'm not making Emily leave. I invited her over."

"Why are you being so hostile?"

"I have a feeling you know why."

"No, I don't. All right, maybe I do. You talked to Maya."

"You gave me her address. You gave me the book to take to her. Then you telephoned her." I heard glasses and plates dinging in the kitchen as Emily continued to make her presence known. Curious as I was about the purpose for his visit, I said nothing. I wanted him to bear the burden of the conversation.

"Well," he said.

"Yes?"

"So I have something to say. Something important."

"Just say it, Harry."

"I just took a phone call from Anthony at Brentwood and Bowers—you know the store?"

I glared. "Of course."

He nodded and cleared his throat. "Listen, I lied, and I stole from Angie." He gave me a wounded puppy look, and it was not attractive on a beer-bellied man in his late forties.

"You destroyed a priceless book. Or *books*. You cut engravings from them, which explains all the empty picture frames on your table at home."

"I feel bad about that. I truly am sorry."

"Why did you come *here?*"

"I want you to give me time to tell Angie on my own, in my own way. I don't want her to hear what I've done from you. Anthony already gave me his word that he wouldn't say anything."

"I'll bet. What about Maya? She was angry at you. Don't you think she might tell Angie? I advised her to come clean."

"Maya has her own reasons to stay quiet."

"Do you mean the plant poisonings?"

From the corner of my eye I saw Emily approach. "Hello there," she said, leaning out the door, wine glasses in her hands. "I'm Emily MacKenzie."

Harry gave her a quick, pinched-lipped smile and then zeroed in on me. His eyes riveted to mine, he was silently telling Emily that she was a nuisance who was interrupting a vitally important conversation.

"Don't mind me," Emily said, heading back to the living room.

"I'm curious," I said. "Why did you steal from Angie?"

With an exaggerated sigh, Harry took a backward step, stuffed his hands in his pants pockets, and said, "I needed the money. Did you know Angie gets sixty percent of the Ivy Cottage profits? Deborah, Maya, and I split the other forty. That's the real reason we couldn't bring Annabel in. Angie got the lion's share of the profits. If we'd brought Annabel in, our shares would have dropped to ten percent each."

"Angie finances the company, so I'm not surprised. That's often how it works, Harry. She stands to lose the most if the company folds. Do you resent her for being the investor?"

"Yes." He whispered the word and glanced in the direction of the living room. How he hated the idea that Emily could be listening.

"And your solution was to sell pages from her most precious books? What did you do, borrow the books, cut out as many prints as you could without being caught, then return the books to her?"

An expression of regret passed over his face. An instant later, it evaporated.

"So Angie would be none the wiser," I went on. "In fact, she'd eliminate you as a suspect since you're so open about borrowing and returning. And you knew she wouldn't flip through each volume and count the pages or peel the books open and search for razor cuts. How many prints and engravings have you taken?"

He dropped his arms and shifted on his feet. "Twenty-seven."

I gasped. That was thousands of dollars' worth—maybe ten thousand.

"I've never, ever taken a whole book."

"She'll be thrilled to hear that. What about teacups or pineapple ornaments from the library? Have you stolen anything like that? Or hid them in her garden?"

"Hide teacups? Don't be ridiculous. Look, just give me time—that's all I'm asking."

"I can't promise you I won't say anything to Angie before you do. She hired me to find out who was stealing from her. If she calls me tonight—"

"You can't give me until tomorrow morning?"

"I can't promise you that, no. Maybe you should go to the police tonight and clear things up."

His eyebrows shot up. Involve the police? It had never occurred to him that Angie might take his stealing that seriously. "We can leave the police out of this. This is between friends, and I can make it up to her. She'd never want me to turn myself in."

"Well, that's for Angie to decide."

"I thought I could count on you for a little sympathy. Janice doesn't know what I did, and I don't want her to know. Haven't you ever made a mistake?"

"How is what you did a mistake? Oops, I cut out an engraving and framed it? You lied to Angie about why you were borrowing her books. You took them only to cut pages from them. You're not working on your garden following the great designs of the past. There's no more design in your garden than there is in mine, and Janice would agree."

"You're as bad as Maya. Just as cold. Maybe colder."

Things were about to turn nasty. Harry had been sure of his persuasive charm, but I wasn't buying what he was selling. He sickened me a bit, and he knew it.

"I won't talk to Angie tonight unless she calls me," I said. "It's late and she needs her rest. But on the off chance she calls, I have to tell her what I know."

"Did *you* kill Deborah?" he hissed. "Maybe the police would like to hear my suspicions. Two can play at this. Are you a murderer, Kate Brewer?"

"Are you a murderer, Harry Jelinek?"

"Um, hello?"

A man's voice jolted me and I wheeled to my right. Holding a pizza box and moving hesitantly toward my door, his eyes shooting from me to Harry and back again, the deliveryman seemed to be calculating whether it was worth his job to come between two people accusing each other of murder.

"Kate Brewer?" he asked.

"That's me. Hang on a sec." I headed into my house and asked Emily to get the pizza while I grabbed money for a tip from my kitchen counter—all the while leaving my front door wide open so the poor delivery guy would feel more at ease being outside with Harry. Once the man took his tip, he made a quick exit.

"We're done here, Harry." I stepped back inside, turned, and put my hand on the doorknob, hoping that if my words didn't convey my meaning, my body language would. "Talk to Angie *tonight*. People tend to be more forgiving when you come forward and admit what you've done without being forced to do so." I shut the door.

"He's the thief?" Emily asked.

Spinning back to her, I said, "One of them. There are at least two. And I'm so hungry I could eat a bear." I glanced toward the kitchen.

"Everything is in the living room," Emily said.

She had already poured two glasses of wine and set plates and napkins on my coffee table. As I flopped to the couch, it struck me that she didn't know the latest on my dual investigations, aside from what Minette had told her. I spent the next few minutes scarfing pizza and filling her in between bites.

"I'm calling Mary Davidson first thing," I finished. "I'll bet she knows something about the thefts."

"Or she knows something about the murder. What if Harry thinks Mary knows something?"

The question sent a jolt through me. What if he did? Or what if Harry knew Mary wanted to talk to me? Worse still, what if he'd driven to Angie's house after we'd talked to persuade Angie not to call the police? What if he were there right now? "Emily," I said, dropping my pizza slice on my plate, "I sent Harry to Angie's house."

"I heard."

"Do you think he would hurt her?"

As Emily chewed, she pondered my question.

"Kate." From her perch on the back of the couch, Minette floated to my shoulder. "Call Angie on the telephone and tell her Harry might be dangerous. Warn her."

"You're right. I don't think he'll do anything with Mary there, but it's best to be safe." I strode to the kitchen and dug my phone out of my purse, scrolling my contacts for Angie's number. Why had Harry come to *my* house? Yes, he'd said it was to ask me for time, but surely Anthony at the shop had told him about Maya being there too. She knew all about his scam. Had he begged *her* for time?

Mary Davidson answered the phone. I could hear a television in the background. Angie had gone to bed early, she said, and she didn't want to disturb her after such an awful day. She'd just turned Harry Jelinek away at the door.

Hearing that, I breathed a sigh of relief. Minette darted into the kitchen, fastened her arms around my forefinger, and laid her head on top of my phone.

"When we talked earlier, I had a feeling you knew something important but didn't want to speak in front of Angie," I said.

The line went silent. After a few seconds, Mary said, "After I told you about Harry and Maya arguing, I remembered something else, but I didn't want to worry Angie with it. She's already stretched to the limit. I was here for last month's tea meeting. Jack was having a confused day and needed extra care. He kept getting up to bang on his bedroom window. When I came downstairs for a Coke, I heard Deborah threatening Annabel. They were in the kitchen and didn't see me."

"What was she threatening her about?"

"Deborah wanted money. *More* money, was the way she put it. She said if she didn't get it, she'd tell Angie what Annabel had done and Annabel would never be part of Ivy Cottage. She said Annabel shouldn't be part of the company anyway, seeing as how she was trying to destroy it."

I sighed. We were back to the pineapple ornaments, though blackmail was a startling new element, and blackmail was always a motive for murder. "Deborah saw Annabel steal a pineapple ornament," I explained. "She must have been blackmailing Annabel over it. I wonder how long that had been going on."

"That wasn't all of it, I'm sure. Deborah did say something like 'that pineapple in your purse,' but she got very angry when she said Annabel was destroying the company, trying to hurt all of them because of her envy and bitterness. I don't know what she meant because Annabel stormed outside after that, but I don't think it fits with stealing a library ornament."

No, it didn't.

CHAPTER 12

B one tired and stuffed to the gills with pizza, I crawled into bed not long after Emily left. I'd updated her on all the latest, and she'd promised to mull things over. Though I'd turned up the central air, the bedroom was still a little warm, so I pushed the comforter my knees. Minette floated in and landed atop its puckers and folds, sitting with her legs straight in front of her, her tiny body sinking a tad into the polyester fluff.

"I think Mary was telling the truth," she said. "I heard it in her voice. Are you tired, Kate?"

"I *am* tired. And I agree, she was telling the truth. I'm glad she was there when Harry showed up. Tell me more about what you saw in Harry's bedroom."

"Are we going to fight Hacquetia?"

"I don't know how, but yes we are. You, me, and Emily." I sighed and rubbed my fingers over my eyes, my mind shifting gears from Deborah's murder to the evil Hacquetia. "You need to tell me more about her. About her weaknesses."

"She is envious," Minette said. "She thinks she's better than any other fairy in the Smithwell Forest, and much better than the foxes and birds."

"So she's full of herself," I said with a nod. Fading quickly, I closed my eyes. "That can be useful. Does her family live in the woods?"

"Her brother, Thornbane."

"That's an unpleasant name."

"He chose it."

"How unusual."

The last thing I remember Minette saying before I drifted off to sleep was, "It's not unusual. He had another name once, but evil chooses new names."

THE NEXT MORNING I rose early, ate a large breakfast, and fixed Minette buttered toast and maple syrup. While she ate at my table and I drank my tea, I promised her again that I would find a way to stop Hacquetia, but I said finding Deborah's killer and telling Angie about her thieving friends had to come first. "So no going to the forest by yourself," I cautioned. "Wait until Emily and I come up with a plan. Then we go together. Until then, stay in the house when you're not with me, and if someone comes to the door, go up the fireplace."

She was satisfied with that, though she didn't understand why I wanted her to hide if someone came to the door, and she was eager to dive into our murder investigation again, but the name Thornbane played in my mind now, unsettling me for some reason. I almost chuckled. Thornbane was a fairy, for goodness' sake. A predator, maybe, but still a tiny fairy.

Minette plopped the last of her buttered toast in her mouth, rubbed her hands on my napkin, and got to her feet. "Who do we question this morning in our investigation?"

"Annabel. She works at the Town Office, and Emily is coming with us."

She cooed and, like a cheerleader, threw her arms over her head. "Emily! Hooray!"

"We may as well see Rancourt, too, since the station is next door to the Town Office. He needs to know about Angie's stolen books and ornaments, not to mention the hidden teacups and marmalade jars in her garden."

"Jack saw someone hide those, but he can't remember who."

"He's sharp when it comes to what he *sees*. It's making sense of what he sees that he has trouble with. I need to talk to Angie too. I wonder if Harry's told her yet about the books he destroyed. He tried to last night, so I'll give him another hour or two before I break the news."

Minette and I hopped into my Jeep, picked up Emily at her house, and drove for downtown Smithwell.

Half a mile down Birch Street, Emily angled back to look at Minette on the rear floor, behind my seat. "I've got a surprise for you." She held out the hem of her aqua-colored summery shirt and pointed to a spacious pocket sewn at the side. "It's deep and airy, and you're welcome to sit in it. There's one on each side of my shirt."

I heard Minette squeak with happiness. "I won't suffocate in the tight Kate jeans!"

"Good idea," I mumbled. "Thanks, Emily."

Minette hurled herself to the roof of the Jeep then swooped down, diving with precision into Emily's left pocket.

"Stay in there," I ordered. "We're almost downtown."

A couple minutes later I found a parking spot on Falmouth Street, Smithwell's main road. The Town Office, a three-story brick Colonial Revival building, was half a block south of us, on the corner of Falmouth and Water.

"You do the talking," Emily said. "Minette and I will keep our mouths shut and listen."

Minette giggled.

"Annabel's going to wonder why you're with me."

"I'm your deputy, working for Angie," Emily said as she unhooked her seatbelt and slid down from her seat. "Annabel won't know the difference. From what you've told me she's not the brightest bulb."

We mounted the Town Office's steps, past the two Doric columns on either side of the entrance and into the cool lobby. "There are only six thousand people in Smithwell, so there can't be that many town employees, right?" I said.

"Never underestimate bureaucracy," Emily replied. "Where do we start?"

We took the elevator to the third floor and made a nuisance of ourselves by peeking into occupied offices, disturbing people at their work. At the last office on the floor, I asked if anyone knew where Annabel Baker worked and received head shakes in reply. We were about to leave when a woman walked by, a tall iced coffee in her hand.

"Did I hear Annabel Baker? She's in Finance, first floor."

We thanked her, took the elevator back down, and found the Finance office after a couple wrong turns. I spotted Annabel immediately. She was standing at a copy machine with her back to us, but her long, dark hair gave her away.

"Annabel?" I said.

I thought she'd fall over when she saw me. "Crud! I *work* here, Kate." She trained her guns on Emily. "Who are you? You don't belong to the garden society."

"I'm working with Kate on her investigation," Emily said flatly.

It was mostly true, I told myself. Not a total lie. Emily, Minette, and I had become quite the team.

Annabel shot me a wounded look. "We talked about this at your house. I *came* to you."

"I want to ask you about something else," I said. "Let's go somewhere for a few minutes."

"Oh, all right, if you'll leave me alone," she groused. "Follow me."

She tossed a sheet of paper from the copier to a desk, grabbed her purse from the back of her chair, and marched out the office door and down the hall. When she reached a corner, she whipped around to face me. "What is it? I've got a lot of work to do. I can't afford to lose this no-good job of mine."

I took that as *I don't have time for preliminaries*, so I got right down to business. "First, Maya isn't the only one who heard from Deborah about the pineapple ornaments you've been taking. Last month, someone else heard—or overheard—her accuse you of putting an ornament in your purse. You can't keep it a secret any longer. The best thing you can do is return all the ornaments you took and apologize to Angie. At least you haven't stolen any of her books. That's what really galls her. You should also tell Angie that you're the one who poisoned her plants."

Annabel made a choking sound.

I wasn't finished shocking her. "Did you do it to pay Angie and the others back for not asking you to join Ivy Cottage?"

"This is nuts! I can't believe you said that to my face!" In a fit of anger, she flung her hands in the air. "Maya told you, right? Well, Maya lied, like she always does. She's a bald-faced liar. She lies about everyone, including herself."

There was no concrete denial in her words, only anger. I'd hit the expected nerve.

"Well, you tell Maya to back off, Kate, or I've got a few secrets of my own to tell. Got it? And then you"—she pointed a finger at me—"mind your own business. You are so far out of line it's not funny. You don't know who you're dealing with."

What a load of bluster. I'd really whacked that nerve. In addition to that, I was throwing a monkey wrench into her plans to join Ivy Cottage should the others ever come to their senses and beg her to partake of their profits. If Angie found out what Annabel had done, she would bar her from joining. Then again, once she learned about Harry and Maya, she'd probably pull her money from the whole enterprise. "Tell Angie about the ornaments and herbicide before I do. Be honest with her and say *why*. Tell her you were hurt, you overreacted, and you'll make up for it somehow. Maybe you can salvage the friendship."

Annabel laughed. "Angie's not my friend. She's too high and mighty to have friends like me."

"You mean a thieves?" Emily said. "How snobbish of her."

Annabel gave her the evil eye. "What's your last name, lady?"

"It's MacKenzie. Mack, not Mick."

"You have to take action to fix what you've done," I said. "And for your information, Angie considers *all* of you her friends. That's why she hired me to help her. She's heartbroken that her *friends* would steal from her and poison her plants. Talk to her. This doesn't have to end up with the police getting involved."

Annabel blinked, flabbergasted to think she might be in serious, police-calling trouble. "Did Angie say she'd report me for killing some plants? Man, oh man. What did I tell you? She's no friend."

There was such a disconnect with this bunch. Somehow it was fine to poison Angie's plants or destroy her priceless books but not fine for Angie to call the police about those things. "The police are already involved. The plants, the books—they're bound to come up in their investigation of Deborah's murder. Detective Rancourt isn't through questioning us."

"Yeah, well I didn't kill Deborah over some stupid ornaments. Maybe Angie or Jack did. Ever think about that?"

With that, Annabel steamed away, flicking her hair over her shoulders. And I decided then and there that I wasn't going to give Harry or Annabel or Maya any more time. After I talked to Rancourt, I'd tell Angie what her so-called friends had done.

"Rancourt next?" Emily said.

"Let me call the station first," I said.

On the second ring, the desk officer answered. Rancourt, he said, was out, but he was due to return at any moment. I hung up without leaving a message.

"Mack not Mick?" I said when we were out on the sidewalk.

"Hey, I wanted Annabel to get the spelling right."

"Let's wait for Rancourt in my car."

We walked half a block to where I'd parked, my mind working the case. Had *all* of Angie's friends carried out some nasty deed intended to hurt her? It was beginning to look like that. But why? To think that yesterday I'd assured her that only one of her friends was responsible. And how did Deborah's murder fit with the whole sordid mess?

Dark gray skies loomed to the west. If the storm didn't evaporate, like so many storms had done lately, we'd finally get some rain.

Emily climbed carefully into my Jeep, holding her shirt out on the left side so Minette wasn't pressed like a sardine between her body and the seat back. "So Kate, how did you know Annabel was the one who killed Angie's plants?"

"It was something Mary Davidson said when I called Angie's house last night."

"Deborah's argument with Annabel?"

"She said Annabel was destroying the company, trying to hurt them all. I took a gamble it was about poisoning the plants used to make their lip balm."

"And Annabel proved you right with her wild reaction."

I gazed ahead, noting a few stray drops of rain spitting against the car's windshield.

"Annabel really is a liar," Minette said.

Her pea-sized hands were gripping the edge of Emily's pocket.

"Are you comfortable in there?" Emily asked.

"Very! Thank you, Emily, my friend. You knew just what I needed to breathe. But Annabel is a liar."

I found my umbrella on the floor of the back seat. "Try telling us something we don't know, Minette."

Emily directed a finger at the windshield. "Here comes Rancourt. Good grief, has the man put on weight? I worry about him. He's positively *waddling*."

"He works hard and doesn't get enough sleep, so cut him some slack," I said, popping my car door open. "You and Minette wait here. He'll be more candid if it's just me."

CHAPTER 13

"Sit down, Kate. I had a feeling you'd stop by today. I must be psychic, huh?" Rancourt invited me to take the small chair in front of his desk, but before sitting himself, he walked to the other side of his office, to a small coffee maker, and poured himself a cup of thick-looking black coffee.

"That's new," I said.

"I needed my own machine. I hate the flavored junk they buy for the office maker."

"What about that thing?" I asked, pointing at the brass light fixture in the middle of his ceiling. It was dusty and dirty, and the ceiling tiles around it were stained, suffering water damage at one point, I supposed.

"Not my territory." He sank into his chair. "Are you still helping Angie Palmer with her friend troubles?"

"That's partly why I'm here. I've uncovered some information that could be helpful."

"I'm all ears."

He drank while I passed on the latest facts, including what Annabel had told me at the Town Office. Whenever his eyebrows arched a speck, I knew I'd offered him something new and potentially useful.

"You left out Maya," he said when I'd finished. "What has she done?"

"Apart from not telling Angie what Annabel and Harry were up to? Good question. She's done something, I'm sure. I need to ask Jack who he saw hiding the marmalade jar in the flower bed near his bedroom window."

A faint smile crossed Rancourt's lips. "Hmm."

"But why would Maya hide Angie's teacups and jars?" I said. "Spite, I suppose. But over what? It's a childish thing to do."

"Yes, but it's safe and easy. It's not like stealing a felony-sized amount of property, which is what Harry Jelinek did."

"Stating the obvious, these people don't like each other. Some of their animosity can be traced to Ivy Cottage and their feeling that Angie doesn't deserve the lion's share of the profits. That's why Harry is selling the prints. He's getting even with Angie for having more money than he does and for earning sixty percent on top of that. He takes his revenge and makes serious money in the process."

"You could be right. We know he's not in any financial or medical difficulty. He didn't need the money, so it could be spite. Getting his own back."

"Maya also wanted Angie's money. She knew about Harry stealing the prints. I think she was pressuring him into cutting her in on the profits when he sold them to Brentwood and Bowers, and that's what they were arguing about in the library when Mary Davidson walked in. Harry was telling her he knows what the buying public wants. He knows the best prints to steal for the biggest profits."

Rancourt upended his cup, draining the contents. "Speculation, but worth my attention."

I slumped in my chair, tired and frustrated with my inability to mesh the clues in both cases. Beginning to grasp the hows and whys of the thefts and poisonings, I was still baffled by Deborah's murder. I'd been so sure her death was connected to

Angie's "friend troubles," as Rancourt had called them, but I was starting to rethink that. "I don't think Annabel would have killed Deborah because she saw her take pineapple ornaments. If it was so important to her that no one find out, she wouldn't have told *me*. That defeats the purpose of killing Deborah, if the purpose was to hide the theft."

"Possibly." Rancourt struggled out of his seat and refilled his cup at the coffee maker.

"Besides, I'm sure Maya heard from Deborah that Annabel had stolen an ornament, but Maya wasn't murdered."

"Neither did she tell Mrs. Palmer who was stealing from her," Rancourt said. Cup in hand, he strolled to his single outside window, his view marred by streaks of rain. "Terrific friends."

I angled around in my chair. "Who had reason to murder Deborah? Annabel says Jack and Deborah didn't get along in the past, that they had bad blood between them. His dementia had to have changed that, you'd think. Whatever passed between the two, he's forgotten about it."

"He can't remember what he did to her." Rancourt turned back to me. "That would infuriate me, and it probably infuriated her. But Jack Palmer wasn't the victim, Deborah Wetherbee was. By the way, Mr. Palmer told me he found the bloody ornament on his bedroom floor. He doesn't know how it got there. He said it was 'out of place.' Seems to be his favorite phrase."

"You're saying Deborah had reason to hate Jack and she was ticked off he couldn't remember that?"

Silence.

"Sounds petty and unreasonable of her."

Rancourt ran a hand down the side of his face. "This is my third cup of coffee, I'm still beat, and the day's far from over."

"What do you know about Deborah's past?"

"I really am beat."

"Detective, I've been very forthcoming."

"As members of the public should be."

"As I always am with you."

"How's Emily's globe-trotting husband? I haven't seen him in a while."

This was maddening. "How's Officer Bouchard? I haven't seen *him* in hours."

"He left this morning. Vacation." Rancourt sipped his coffee and gave me a serene smile. "I hear that Deborah Wetherbee used to teach at the University of Maine in Farmington. Didn't you go there?"

"You know I'm from Ohio."

"Oh yeah, that's right. But you've lived in Maine for twenty years, haven't you?"

"Close to twenty-one."

"Then again, by Maine standards, you're a newcomer."

Our nonsensical conversation was interrupted by the arrival of a sergeant, who left folders for Rancourt on his desk and told him he envied his personal coffee maker but that he really should get one of those pod machines and leave the basket-era makers behind.

Rancourt ignored him. "Thanks for stopping by, Mrs. Brewer. I'll call if I need anything else. Don't forget your umbrella."

He was dismissing me and, worse, ignoring the information I'd brought him. I rose from my chair, a few choice words on the tip of my tongue.

"And thank you, Sergeant," Rancourt said, "but I'm afraid if I had one of those, everyone in the office would want to use it. Keep it plain and unappealing, that's my motto."

Yet Rancourt wasn't dismissive—at least toward me. And he was no fool. I pondered those two facts as I walked back to my

Jeep. By the time I'd climbed inside, I'd deciphered our strange conversation.

"Emily, can you text Laurence and ask him if he can find out about Deborah Wetherbee's time at the University of Maine at Farmington? She used to teach there, but I don't know when."

She dug out her phone. "This has to do with her murder?"

"Yes. Do you think Laurence knows someone who knew her at Farmington?"

Emily smiled. It was a rhetorical question, she knew. Laurence, who used to travel to American embassies around the world for "government work"—that was how Emily described his employment—was now in worldwide "hotels and construction," whatever that meant. It was a puzzle to me. What I knew for certain was this: Doors opened at the drop of his name, and not just because people liked him. Though they did. As long as we didn't ask him to divulge sensitive information or his sources, he was eager to help. I think he enjoyed the idea of his wife solving crimes, and he liked to encourage her in it. Perhaps it was now a shared passion, this sniffing out wrong-doers. Because I was pretty sure Laurence had been a spook—a spy pursuing international evildoers. And maybe he still was.

"He'll call as soon as he knows," Emily said, sliding her phone back in her purse. He said it's vital to examine the victim's past and he wondered when we'd get around to that.

"We should have done it yesterday," I said. The skies were darker now, and thunder, previously in the distance, rolled nearer. Looking out my windshield at the falling rain, I turned the sole of my attention to Deborah's death. I had carried out Angie's tasks regarding the thefts and plant vandalism to the best of my ability, though a couple loose threads remained, and was grudgingly coming to the conclusion that Deborah's murder was unconnected to those events.

I had to hand it to Rancourt. He'd provided me with an avenue of inquiry, I'm sure with reciprocity in mind, and he'd done so in what he could later claim was complete innocence. *I was only chatting with a helpful member of the public. All I said was the victim taught at what I thought was her alma mater, the University of Maine.*

Her voice somewhat muffled by Emily's pocket, Minette spoke up. "I'm hungry now. I didn't have very much toast for breakfast."

"Aww, poor thing," Emily murmured. "Can we eat somewhere? Let's get Italian sandwiches and Minette can have our parsley."

"Soon," I said. "Angie's house first. I want to tell her what I discovered about her books and plants. And maybe talk to Jack again."

"I don't know how he can help," Emily said.

"Deborah saw Annabel steal a library ornament, but she said nothing to Angie, though she probably told Maya."

"It's true," Minette said.

"Maya knew about Harry destroying valuable books," I went on, "but again, she said nothing to Angie. None of them like Angie much, or like each other. What did they think of Deborah? In his fawning way, Harry liked to compliment her. He called her the 'master cook,' though Annabel said that was because no one else wanted to do her drudge work."

"You said she used her own kitchen," Emily said.

"Imagine the smell and mess."

"But she received only thirteen percent of the profits. Now Harry and Maya will split her percentage."

"I don't think so, Emily. They have to find another cook and offer him or her at least Deborah's share."

"They are *selfish*," Minette said. Her hands were fists, digging into the hem of Emily's pocket, and her voice had taken on a raspy tone I'd never heard before. "Like Hacquetia, they are selfish."

"What have you heard that could help?" I asked her. "What else did you hear Jack say besides 'that sneaky cat'? I don't even know what that means. Was he referring to Mary? One of Angie's friends? Is it a woman—or a man, maybe?"

"I'm thinking about it," she answered. "I need more information, Kate. And I need *food*."

"You're supposed to have a fairy's intuition. That's why you're here with us, taking a risk someone will see you."

Minette's wings expanded, filling Emily's ample pocket, and then rose above her head, and for the umpteenth time since we'd met, she said, "My hearing is exceptional, Kate."

"For once hearing has nothing to do with it. We've all heard the same things, except for when you were in Jack's room. Which you shouldn't have been, I hasten to add. I'm tired of trying to keep you safe, but especially when there's no purpose to you putting yourself in danger. You're not helping with the case, you're just making trouble."

Suddenly the rain picked up again, drumming hard on the Jeep's hood. I dug my keys out of my jeans pocket. From the corner of my eye, I saw Emily watching me.

"Angie's house," I said, starting the engine.

CHAPTER 14

"Angie won't be long and you're welcome to wait for her," Mary said. She ushered us inside and shut the front door, though not before pausing to relish the scent of rain striking Smithwell's heretofore dry earth. "Just smell that! It's heavenly!"

I introduced Emily, then the two of us followed Mary from the front room into the library, where Mary offered to make us coffee and bring us a snack. I said yes to the snack but declined the coffee. Emily asked for a mugful of it. Using Angie's largest mug, please.

"I wouldn't bother you or Angie, but I have some news for her," I said, taking the same seat I had when I'd talked to Jack.

"News to do with the recent events in this house?" Mary clasped her hands in front of her, worry creeping into her voice. "I hope it's good news. Angie needs some about now."

"It is and it isn't. It's the information she wanted, but it will upset her."

"I think I see. Excuse me."

Mary went to the kitchen—I soon smelled coffee brewing—and Emily began to peruse the books on the shelves. When she came to one of the pineapple ornaments, she lifted it, turning to me as she gauged its weight. "Heavy," she mouthed.

Minette's head popped above Emily's left-hand pocket. A second later, she soared from the pocket to a shelf near Emily's head. I kept my lips zipped. I was through warning her about danger. Through taking her with me when I left the house, frankly. Maybe I'd start again in September, when I could wear a sweater or light jacket, but for the remainder of the summer, she could stay at home.

"I'll be back," I told Emily, walking off for the kitchen.

Mary was arranging small cookies on a plate when I entered. I wanted to talk more about Jack and Angie's friends, and Mary agreed to do so, as long as we stopped when Angie came home. I asked if she'd ever overheard another argument between Angie's friends, aside from the two arguments she'd told me about.

"Little arguments, all the time. Stop staring at the lemon cookies and have one."

I dropped to a stool, took a cookie, and ate the whole thing in one bite.

"Hungry?"

"Starving, actually."

"They're always sniping at each other like kids." She took more cookies from the refrigerator, put them on the plate, and carried on with her impression of the group, shaking her head like a disappointed parent. "Maya's the worst. That woman is primed to go off like an incendiary device. You've probably noticed there isn't much you can say to her without causing some imagined offense, and I *do* mean imagined. She loves to argue."

"So why is she friends with Angie? Angie's not like that."

"They're business partners and members of the same garden society. You know how clubs and money throw people together who ordinarily wouldn't dream of rubbing elbows."

"What about the others? Why do they come for tea and pretend to be friends?"

"Some of them might be friends, in a way. Maybe, could be." Mary retrieved a pint carton of cream from the refrigerator and tore several sheets of paper towels from a holder on the counter, laying them on a tray before going on. "They can be friendly when they're talking about flowers and gardening. I'm still amazed Angie hired you to find out which one of them was stealing from her. *Did* you find out?"

"At least two of them were stealing," I replied. "I'm sure Angie will tell you after I tell her. She may not allow them in the house again."

"Two of them, that's unbelievable," she groused, her eyes drifting past me to a distant spot over my shoulder. "When did Angie get pink butterflies?"

I spun around. "Where?"

"It's gone now. It was huge, like an atomic-blast science-fiction-movie butterfly. They die in the house and I have to sweep them up."

In an attempt to distract Mary—I knew precisely what she'd seen, and I was furious with Minette—I took another cookie and asked her for the recipe.

"They come in the mailbox," she said.

"The cookies?"

"The butterflies. Mail-order insects. Angie likes the brightly colored ones best. Some of them aren't native to New England and might be illegal to import, for all I know." She poured a cup of coffee and put it on the tray. "Here we go. Your friend must wonder what's happened to us."

"She's enjoying the library," I said, walking behind Mary, searching for Minette, and fuming that she'd let herself be seen.

As Mary slid a lamp out of the way and set the tray on one of two round tables in the library, Emily took the opportunity to play mime with me—pointing at her pocket, making finger-fluttering motions with her hand, helplessly shrugging her shoulders.

Mary turned and Emily grinned. "Thank you so much. I didn't expect all this."

"Try one of the lemon cookies," I said. "Mary, how long has Jack been doing so poorly?"

"Unfortunately, the last six months have been a rapid downhill slide."

Emily took her coffee but remained standing, walking about the library, now and then angling her head for a better look at the spines of old, ornate volumes.

I retook my seat. "But he still knows what he's seeing, and he seems to know when something isn't normal, even if he forgets the details."

"I think so. If you catch him in a lucid moment."

"For instance, he knew the pineapple ornament you brought him didn't belong in his bedroom, but he forgot he asked for it and you gave it to him."

Mary nodded thoughtfully and took a seat across the room. "That's Jack. Bits and pieces of life, some of it real, some of it . . . well, not *unreal*, but not filtered correctly. When I give him his medication, he doesn't think it's strange, but he's positive I just gave it to him, though it may have been four or six hours ago, and sometimes when I bring him lunch, he asks me why I'm bringing lunch again. He swears he ate ten minutes ago."

"Jack told me Angie's friends creep around the house like cats. What do you think he means?"

She crossed her legs and relaxed, not minding my questions now, it seemed. "He *sees* them. He must because doesn't have hallucinations. When he said that, did he sound irritated?"

"Yes. He said he shoos them away, and I got the feeling he thought they were snooping around the house or were in a room they shouldn't be in. Does Jack come out of his room much?"

"He does, and I encourage him to do that. It's essential he stays physically active. Angie and I are planning to move him to a room on the first floor, though, so he doesn't take the stairs. He's good on them now, but he won't be in a month. Still, that's stalling the inevitable. It won't be long before he can't live at home." Mary furrowed her brow and leaned forward in her seat. "Could Jack have seen who killed Deborah Wetherbee? Is that what you're getting at?"

"Not the murder, but maybe something leading up to it. If he'd seen the murder—"

"He would've said so," Mary interrupted. "He'd speak up about seeing a violent attack. He wouldn't forget it."

"I hate to interject this," Emily said, taking the library's third chair, "but have we fully considered whether Jack killed Deborah? He doesn't like Angie's friends, and if his mind is going . . ."

"It's not possible," Mary said. "He's easy to blame because he can't defend himself, but he's not capable."

"He could have hit Deborah without knowing the damage he was inflicting," Emily argued.

"That violence and blood?" Mary said. "God help us all if dementia makes for vicious killers. No, Jack couldn't and wouldn't."

I tended to agree with Mary, and I said so. Evil has nothing to do with memory, intelligence, or anything of the sort, I thought. It's a problem of the soul, not the brain. Then again, what did I know about the state of Jack Palmer's soul? Could he have been a killer at heart *before* dementia robbed him of his memories?

"Does Jack ever forget who Angie is?" Emily asked.

"Sure, sometimes," Mary said.

That threw me. "So Angie could be one of the 'cats' he complains about?"

"I guess so."

"Jack could know something important." More than that, I thought, Jack could be the key. If only we could trust his version of the facts. The doorbell sounded, shaking me from my thoughts. Mary excused herself.

Emily swatted my arm and hissed, "I couldn't stop her from going upstairs."

"Leave her," I said. "Let her figure out how to get back to my car."

"What if Mary sees her? Aren't you worried?"

"Of course, but I can't keep telling her to stay out of sight. Maybe she needs to be trapped in this house overnight before she gets the message."

Harry burst into the library, Mary close behind, and in the space of one second he sized up the situation. Me and Emily waiting, Mary playing host to us both until Angie arrived. He aimed his wrath at me. "You couldn't wait a few more hours? Let me talk to her before you do, I'm asking you. You owe me that."

"I don't owe you anything, Harry, but I'll let you talk to Angie first. Then I'll tell her what I know because I most certainly do owe *her*."

Mary held up a finger. She started to say something to Harry, then stopped. Then grimaced. Comprehension was dawning.

Harry was a cad, and he was here to make a confession. "I may as well get more coffee," she said, her tone indignant.

Like Maya and Annabel, Harry continued to blame me for his own misbehavior. Neck stiff, his face a mask of anger, he glared at me as he leaned on a bookcase.

Emily, as she was inclined to do, noted the irony. "My, my, if looks could kill. Did you steal from Angie too, Kate? Destroy valuable belongings? You must have done something terribly wrong." She took a noisy sip of coffee.

"Have a lemon cookie, Harry," I said.

"No, thanks."

When the doorbell rang again, Mary huffed loudly—enough to be heard in the library—and I felt sorry for her. Jack was her responsibility, not all of us, and taking care of him was more than enough work for one woman.

Seconds later, Maya strode into the library, her eyes saucers when she saw Harry.

"I'll be back with *more* coffee," Maya called out.

"What's this?" Maya snapped. "Here to borrow another book, are you? Run out of money? Or are you here to tell Angie I murdered Deborah?"

"If you want to know," Harry said, "I think you did kill Deborah. So there you have it."

Maya stiffened her back and gave him an arrogant grin. "So there you have it? That doesn't cut it, Harry. Idiot cliches are not admissible in court."

"Where were you when we left the greenhouse?" Harry fired back. "Kate went with Angie, I went with Annabel. Where did you go?"

"I went to look at Angie's calendula, like she told me to, and then the chamomile."

"The chamomile you poisoned?" Harry said, grinning smugly.

I cleared my throat, drawing their attention. "Annabel poisoned the chamomile."

Harry's jaw dropped.

Maya roared with laughter. "Oh, you—you jerk—you thought I did it? Is that what you told Angie?"

"None of you told Angie anything," I said. "Not a single one of the people she called friends let her know what was happening."

Maya ignored me. "We use that chamomile in our lip balm, Harry. No way I'd ruin the company I've worked so hard to build."

"You can always find chamomile," Harry said, "but sticking it to Angie and her garden is priceless, no? And that was always your goal." Changing his mind about the lemon cookies, he strode to the tray, snatched two of them, and shoved one in his mouth.

"Free chamomile?" Maya shot back. "We get it free from Angie, dumbo. If you've found another source, I'd love to hear about it. It's not cheap on the open market, you know."

Harry was bristling with anger, chewing furiously. "I've forgotten more than you'll ever know about business. Now let's talk about *you* and the things you've done." He spat cookie crumbs with each word and didn't stop to wipe his mouth. "Start with what you're doing here. Your hands aren't clean, Maya."

"I'm here to protect myself," she said. "Kate threatened me. Isn't that right, Kate? All I did was hide a few of Angie's things to drive her nuts."

"Harry, you've said you and Annabel walked to the house together after leaving the greenhouse, but you separated at some point. Annabel found Deborah before you did. Where did you go? Where did *she* go?"

"She came here, to the library, and I went to the restroom, not that it's your business."

Maya snickered.

"Where she went after that, I don't know, because I didn't see her again until she howled like a stuck pig."

"Can we stop this now?" Mary said, entering the library with a packed tray—more coffee, more cookies, and what looked like leftover pastries from our tea the day before. As she positioned the tray on the library's second table, the doorbell chimed once more. For an instant she didn't move, she simply stared down at the tray.

"Mary, would you like me to get that?" I asked.

"No, thank you. Everyone, eat. If you're eating, you're not arguing, and if you're not arguing, you're not waking Mr. Palmer. And if you wake Mr. Palmer, *I'll* be the one doing some killing."

For the third time since my arrival, Mary trudged off to answer the front door.

I got up to snag myself a pastry, and when I returned to my chair, I decided to ask an incendiary question in spite of Jack napping away upstairs. "Harry, I'd like you to tie a loose end for me. Did you ever take entire books from this library, or did you only cut prints from books and then return them?"

Harry looked as though I'd struck him in the face.

"I ask because Angie is missing whole books, too, not just parts of them. I know Maya hid some in the flower beds, but I—"

"There you go again," Maya protested. "You have no proof."

"Yet you're here to talk to Angie, and so is Harry," I said, smiling and digging into my pastry. I *was* starving, after all.

Mary halted at the door to the library, and in a deadpan voice said, "The gang's all here" before waving Annabel Baker in ahead of her. "I'll put *more* coffee on. Eat now. *Please*."

CHAPTER 15

"Did Kate bully you too?" Maya asked Annabel.

"I don't know if bully is the word," she answered. "Warned, maybe. I came here to apologize for what I did."

Maya smirked. "What a good, good girl."

"You're not blameless yourself," Annabel said.

A flash of light was followed quickly by a loud crack of thunder, jolting me in my seat. I twisted back to see rain cascading over what must have been cracks in the gutters over the library windows.

"That'll wake Jack up," Emily said.

I nodded and finished off my pastry as I listened to Maya, Annabel, and Harry argue. Mary had returned with her own cup of coffee and seemed on the verge of telling them all to leave. They debated which one of them was the worst of the three. Maya and Annabel concurred that it was Harry. In a purely financial sense, that was true. He'd robbed Angie of thousands of dollars and irreparably damaged valuable books she loved. But what deep spite had led Maya to hide books and teacups and marmalade jars in Angie's flower bed?

Furthermore, did any of that matter anymore?

I cut their argument short. "None of this has anything to do with Deborah's murder."

"Don't start," Harry said.

Emily's phone rang. She left the library for the front room before answering it. From what few words I heard, it was Laurence on the line.

Lightning flashed hard, and I steeled myself against the thunderclap.

"Sheesh!" Annabel cried. "It's right over us!"

Mary gazed at the ceiling, as though she could see Jack through it, rising from his bed, confused or even frightened by the storm. "I'll be back," she said, making for the staircase.

Without asking if she minded, I followed her up the stairs. She didn't object.

Jack was awake but drowsy, and he smiled at us both when we entered. "I remember you," he said to me.

"I love these moments," Mary said, picking up a fallen throw blanket from beside his bed. "I mean, when he remembers and enjoys. They're precious."

"Hi, Jack," I said. "I'm Kate. You're right—we talked yesterday."

"Are you hungry?" Mary asked him. She folded the throw and laid it at the foot of the bed.

"Cookies would be fine," he said.

"I've got your favorite."

"You go ahead, Mary," I told her. "I'll keep Jack company."

Mary took a half-empty glass from his bedside table and headed for the kitchen, but rather than sit in the chair on the other side of Jack's bed, I began to give his room the once-over, looking for Minette. "Are there any butterflies up here? Pretty ones?"

"How did you know? There was a pretty one over there."

He pointed a bony finger at a four-drawer dresser.

I spotted a pink and ivory wing poking from behind a silver photo frame. Then a tiny hand gripping the frame. Then a face.

Minette gazed up at me, her expression innocence itself. Boy, were we going to have a talk. I tugged at my jeans pocket and motioned at it with a nod of my head. "Jack, what's that?" I said, pointing in the opposite direction.

He looked and Minette dove head-first into my pocket.

"What, my dear? Do you mean the painting?"

"Never mind. I thought I saw something."

Lying to an old friend with dementia. I felt awful. But Jack seeing Minette and me lying about *that* would be a worse offense.

There was another burst of lightning, and the crash of thunder that followed rattled the room's windowpanes.

"I love storms," Jack said. "I always have."

I took the chair by his bed. "I love them too. Can you tell me something, Jack? Why do you bang on that window sometimes?" I called his attention to the window facing the back garden.

"It's like a telephone. It's how I contact people when they're outside and I'm not." He sounded like a little boy explaining something any adult with half a brain should already know. He made me smile.

"So when you need to get someone's attention, you bang on the window."

Wide awake now, he hoisted himself higher on his pillows. "When I see cats prowling in the garden, too."

"Have you ever seen these cats drop things in the flower beds?"

He grinned. "You know them!"

Mary returned with a plate of cookies and a glass of milk for Jack and put them on his bedside table. "Angie just came home, Jack. She'll be up here soon to say hello, as soon as she says hello to the people in the library."

Jack gave me a tip of his chin. "We've been talking about cats in the garden."

"And why Jack bangs on the window sometimes," I added.

"Oh, that's easy," Mary said. "He signals me or Angie, don't you, Jack?" As an aside to me, she said, "We had to lock the windows for safety. They don't open, but I'm afraid he might break the glass one day."

He grinned with satisfaction. "It's a telephone. When I need something or when I see something where it doesn't belong, I hit it."

"Something where it doesn't belong," I repeated.

"Now you have it!"

"Do those cats belong?"

"You *are* clever. Not one bit, they don't."

I leaned toward him and he responded in kind. We were buddies, letting each other in on secrets. "Do you remember banging on the window yesterday? The day you found the pineapple ornament in your bedroom?"

Confusion wrinkled Jack's brow. "Maybe. Was that yesterday? I know that cat was in here when I hit the window. She's a sneaky one. Has been for years. Some things never change."

"Who's sneaky?" Mary asked.

Hearing a rap on the bedroom's open door, I turned to see Emily frantically waving at me with her phone.

I excused myself and stepped outside the door. Not satisfied with that, Emily pulled me down the hall and into a bathroom. "That was Laurence, and you won't believe it," she said, pushing the door shut with her back. "Deborah Wetherbee was an archaeology professor at Farmington until Jack Palmer torpedoed her career. She put in an application for tenure, and he saw to it that the committee denied her. She moved on from Farmington, but she never made tenure."

"When was this?"

"Thirteen years ago."

"She couldn't have carried a grudge for that—"

"Yes, yes, Emily," Minette said, worming out of my pocket and flitting to her shoulder. "Jack remembers sometimes. He calls her 'the cat.'"

"He calls everyone the cat," I said.

"Laurence says denial of tenure is a death sentence for any academic career, and this happened at a time when tenure was easier to obtain. It must have been traumatic for her." Emily lowered her voice to a faint whisper. "Jack accused her of sexually harassing two male students."

"Yikes."

Minette grabbed a fistful of Emily's hair and pulled. "Listen to me!"

Emily yelped and threw back her head, striking the door. "For goodness' sake!"

"Hello in there? Are you all right?"

"Angie," I mouthed.

"I'm fine," Emily said. "Be out in a minute."

I waited until I heard heels clacking down the hall, moving in the direction of Jack's bedroom, before I spoke. "Minette, how do you know Jack remembers Deborah? Does he talk to himself?"

"He talked to *me*. I hid and asked him questions while everyone was fighting downstairs. He didn't mind that he couldn't see me. He called me his magic friend. He likes to talk and doesn't get to talk enough. He's very sad about that."

I put my ear to the door, listening for signs of a continued argument, but all I heard was rain hammering the roof.

"Jack doesn't always remember her," Minette said, "but he said she was the worst cat in the house and she comes to his room.

Yesterday she laughed at him and told him he was going to die soon and she was glad."

Emily grimaced. "Evil."

"Kate, listen." Minette thrashed her wings, pushed off Emily's shoulder, and flew to mine. "Jack said the bad cat came into his room and he used the telephone to tell someone so they'd take her away and she'd stop saying he was going to die."

My heart sank. "Oh no. Not Jack. Please say he didn't."

A look of resignation spread across Emily's face.

"I don't believe it," I said. This gentle man, his eyes glistening with humor, happy to have a magic friend to talk to, bludgeoned a woman to death? Even a woman who cackled in his face and wished for his death? It ran contrary to my every instinct.

I replayed the events of that day in my mind, starting with our departures from the greenhouse. Harry and Annabel walking together toward the house, Deborah and Maya plodding off in different directions, me and Angie talking in the garden. Jack hitting the window, and then, before Angie had time to climb the stairs to his room, Jack dropping the drapes. Letting them fall as he turned away from the window. Because Deborah was already in his room, tormenting him. That's why he'd hit the window, alerting Angie. Deborah, the nasty cat, was where she didn't belong. "We need to leave this bathroom."

Minette lunged for Emily's spacious shirt pocket and I slowly opened the door. Angie and Mary were chatting down the hall—from Jack's room, it seemed—and downstairs Harry was whining about having waited long enough to talk to Angie.

We slipped out the door and crept back downstairs. As soon as I set foot in the library, Annabel lit into me, accusing me of telling Angie about the plants she'd killed, not allowing her a chance to confess and explain herself.

"I haven't talked to Angie," I said. "And by the way, did Deborah try to blackmail you over the plants?"

Annabel blanched. "How did you know?"

I grabbed yet another lemon cookie. "You all have time to talk to Angie."

"Golly, thanks," Maya said.

The three library chairs had been nabbed by Angie's friends, so I stood near the bookcases, next to Emily. At that point I couldn't have cared less about Harry, Annabel, and Maya, except that I wanted Angie to know what sort of friends she had. My thoughts were centered on Jack and trying to wrap my mind around the probability that he was a killer. I envisioned him turning from the window, taking hold of the pineapple ornament Mary had brought him, and . . .

That was as far as my imagination would take me.

Did Angie know Deborah had been denied tenure because of Jack? She must have. So had she invited the woman into her home thinking the past was past and in Jack's current state no one could wish him ill? Did Angie suspect Jack had killed Deborah? What if she'd seen him at the top of the stairs after he'd killed Deborah? She loved him with all her heart. Would she have told him to drop the ornament and forget about the cat at the foot of the stairs?

". . . all Angie's fault, when it comes down to it," Maya was saying.

I perked up.

"She takes sixty percent and we do all the work," she went on. "And our meetings—why do we always come here? Even in a snowstorm, we have to come to *Angie's* house. Angie and more Angie, it's all about Angie."

"She has to watch Jack," I pointed out. "It makes sense she'd want the meetings here."

"Mary can watch him," Maya said.

Harry was nodding his agreement with Maya. "Just *once* we could meet at my house or your apartment. And I'll tell you something else. I'm the marketing expert, but she vetoes designs. What does she know about what sells? She thinks her sixty percent gives her the right to run everything."

Maya gave a small shake of her head. "All our work, all our hard work. No wonder we reacted the way we did, Harry."

The self-justification was nauseating, but I held my tongue.

"You're very quiet, Annabel," Harry said.

Annabel was twirling a strand of dark hair in her fingers, her eyes roaming the library, avoiding Harry and Maya's gaze. "I think you're wrong, Harry. And you too, Maya. You don't work that hard, and it's Angie's money. It's her retirement money. You couldn't have started the company without her." There was genuine sadness in her voice. "What was I thinking, doing that to her chamomile? I poisoned some plants in her greenhouse too. Angie's been nice to me."

"Don't go all wishy-washy on us," Harry said. "You knew what you were doing, and you knew what we were doing."

"At first, I didn't know, but I figured it out," Annabel said. She dropped her hair and shifted in her seat. "Kate, Angie isn't going to stay friends with us, is she?"

Honesty was called for. "Probably not. But I think she may forgive you, and you—"

I was interrupted by Harry's bray of laughter.

"Harry doesn't think he needs forgiveness," Annabel said. Bolder now, she straightened her back and regarded Harry without flinching. "But we all need it."

"Harry's going to need a lawyer more than forgiveness," I said.

That wiped the grin from his face. I thought he might cross the library and smack me.

Angie whipped through the library door, Mary on her heels. "What is going on? Jack's riled up and won't sleep. Kate, why are they here? Everyone tell me the truth and tell me *now*. Kate?"

CHAPTER 16

A ngie had planted herself in the library, refusing to move until she heard the truth, and I'd stayed to make sure that truth was told. Her friends—by now, former friends—had confessed, Harry last and most reluctantly.

When Harry finished his tragic recitation, followed by a plea for mercy, I realized the depth of Angie's sorrow. Her fears had been confirmed, and despite what she'd said to me, she had held out hope that her friends were innocent. Hoping she would go easiest on Annabel, I resolved to tell her later that she was the one friend who truly regretted her actions.

The three former friends left the house, the sky still spitting rain, and Emily waited for me by the front door while I spoke to Angie. Her eyes were rimmed in red, and she blinked to keep new tears from gathering. "I'm so sorry," I said. "Deborah was no friend either."

"Don't be sorry," she replied. "I wanted to know. At least the stealing will stop. That bothered me most of all. My beautiful gardening books."

"Will you report Harry to the police?"

"I haven't decided yet." She drew a deep breath. "I owe you some orchids."

"Later. I'll stop by, or you come visit me. Take the rest of the day off."

"Maybe I'll do that."

"Can I say goodbye to Jack? He remembers me today."

"He'd like that. Mary's up there now."

I climbed the stairs to the second floor, deliberating the pros and cons of telling Angie that Jack may have killed Deborah. But what was the point of that? He would soon end up in a nursing home. Why put Angie through more hell? Walking down the hall for his room, I could hear Mary telling him she had to leave now but she'd be back later, and Angie, his wife, would bring him an egg salad sandwich in a minute. Jack said, "Marvelous!"

I rapped on the open door. "I thought I'd say goodbye to Jack."

"Jack, it's Kate, come to say goodbye," Mary said in her motherly tone. "He's been telling me about a talking butterfly in his room."

Jack was sitting up in bed, his fingers laced across his wide belly. I sat down next to his bed. "Talking butterflies are the best. They're magical friends."

"You understand! I knew you would. What would we do without magic friends? I hope you have some."

"I have one." I was *aching*. How could I turn this man over to Rancourt? I knew Rancourt would have pity on him and treat him as gently as he could, but he'd arrest him all the same. Yet wasn't the truth about murder of the highest importance? Keeping still about what I suspected could not be an option. "Jack, remember the sneaky cat who came into your room yesterday?"

"She was a nasty cat. Said she knew me, but I don't remember her. Said she would ruin my life." His eyebrows shot up. "How is that possible when I don't even know her?"

Mary sank to the end of his bed, removed her glasses, and pinched the bridge of her nose. "Can you tell us which cat this was?"

"The nasty-minded one." He sat forward. "She said she was tired of cooking all the time, which is a strange thing to say. And she came right up to my face, like a vicious cat." He smiled contentedly and relaxed into his pillow. "But she was taken care of. She'll never, ever come back."

Mary slipped her glasses back on and stared at Jack. "No, don't. Don't say that, please. You didn't. You're too good a man."

"Thank you, miss. You're a good woman."

"Taken care of?" That was a funny way to put it. I took Jack's hand in mine and fixed my eyes on his. "You say she was *taken care of.* What do you mean?"

"Taken care of by the other cat, of course." Suddenly his face lit up, and he pointed toward the bedroom door. "That one! She lives here and brings me sandwiches. She stopped that nasty cat in her tracks. I remember now! She hit her good."

Angie stood in the doorway holding a plate. Jack's egg salad sandwich.

"Oh, Lord," Mary said, rising from the bed.

"It's all right," Angie said. "Please don't be afraid." She put the plate on Jack's dresser and turned to face us. I'd never seen such anguish in another woman's eyes. "You can call the police, Mary. I won't leave, and I won't lie. It's still hard for me to fathom, but I killed Deborah. I did. I didn't plan it, but I hit her and she fell down the stairs. I haven't slept since then."

Mary hugged the walls as she made her way to the door, giving Angie a wide berth.

Now it was becoming clearer. "When you came inside to see Jack, Deborah was here, threatening him," I said.

"Deborah was an evil woman, Kate. More evil than my other three friends put together. I'm afraid I haven't chosen my friendships well."

"Did you know Deborah was denied tenure because of Jack's accusation?"

"It wasn't an accusation, it was the truth, and the committee knew it. They found out he was right and let her go quickly. But it was also *thirteen* years ago. When Deborah asked to join the Smithwell Garden Society, I was pleased, really. Maybe we could be civil, even be friends one day. And when Harry suggested her for Ivy Cottage and she agreed, I thought Deborah wanted to move on, leave the past behind. What she really wanted was to come to my house as often as she could and torment my Jack. I honestly didn't think he'd remember her being in his room yesterday."

"Why didn't you just tell Deborah she wasn't welcome?"

"I didn't know what she was doing when she talked to Jack. I thought she was making her peace or talking flowers. How stupid could I be? Why wouldn't she make peace after all he's suffered? Wasn't it time? And yesterday she said she would ruin him and he would die a horrible death soon. That's what she was hissing in his face when I walked in. Jack hadn't even made it all the way back to bed. He was trying to get in and at the same time pull the covers up—to shield himself. She was terrorizing him. Can you understand that?"

"Regardless of her threat, she couldn't have ruined him."

Angie sat down on Jack's bed, in the same place Mary had sat. She wasn't going to fight me or run. Not in front of Jack. She smiled at him and held his hand—two aging hands clasped in love. "Deborah might have done anything, a woman like that. Sent the police here to question him, or worse. My time with him is so short and I love him so much. He's been a good husband. I wasn't going to let her steal days from us. I've said I can't believe what I did, but I don't regret it. Not terribly much, anyway."

Angie wasn't a murderer at heart, but she loved her husband more than life and couldn't let him suffer one iota more than he already had. She would not allow a woman from his past to hound him for something he could no longer remember. The sight of Jack cowering under Deborah's verbal attacks must have sent her over the edge. What would I have done had I found someone tormenting my Michael as he lay dying of cancer?

"But not murder, Angie," I murmured. "Not that."

She nodded. "There aren't many things more sinful. And now I'll have to leave Jack anyway. My worst fear come true. But I've made plans for what future he has left. He doesn't remember me often, so it's all right if I don't see him again. And he likes Mary. She'll take care of him until he has to go to a nursing home." She stifled a sob. "I think that might be very soon."

"Don't cry," Jack said. "I don't like it when people cry."

Angie sniffed. "Yes, yes. I'll stop now. There's no need to cry." When she rose to get his sandwich, he grinned at me, saying, "Will I talk to my magic friend again?"

"I'll make sure you do."

"Oh, you're a nice woman."

RANCOURT AND AN OFFICER I'd never met arrived a few minutes later, as Jack, happily unaware of all that had transpired, ate his lunch and Angie told him how beautifully her late summer roses were blooming. Rancourt thanked me for helping with another case—and in "record time"—though the solution to Deborah's murder had all but fallen into my lap. "Thank Laurence and Jack," I said. "They're the ones. And if Angie decides to report vandalism or thefts at her house and needs a witness, let me know."

"So that matter is resolved?" Rancourt asked.

"Yes, I don't think Angie will take it further. She knows who stole from her and poisoned her plants, and that's enough. Her mind is on Jack."

"And her legal troubles, I think."

I said my goodbyes, and Emily and I headed home in my Jeep. I gave Emily the bare-bones details of what had gone down in Jack's bedroom, filling in the parts she'd missed before she'd padded to the top of the stairs and heard Angie for herself. After that, we were silent as we drove back to Birch Street.

Minette, too, was quiet as a mouse on the way home, stowed away on the floor of the back seat, safe from my fury. She had ignored all my warnings and *talked* to Jack. Ridiculous! Because of Jack's dementia things had turned out well, but that sort of nonsense couldn't continue. I'd turned my life upside down for her since last October, and I was about to do so again as I devised a battle plan to combat Hacquetia and her crew. She owed it to me to be careful.

I dropped Emily off at her house, and Minette stayed on the floor of my Jeep's back seat until I parked in my dooryard, at which point she flew into my pocket. "It's tight in there," I said sarcastically.

"I can breathe okay, Kate."

"Heavens, what a relief."

The rain had stopped and the air was fresh and sweet, but though that usually lifted my spirits, a profound sadness began to settle over me. My feet felt as though they were made of lead as I walked into my kitchen and dropped my purse on the table.

The only saving grace in the whole Palmer affair was that Jack would never be aware of Angie's crime. In fact, he'd never notice her absence. Never miss her. He was by all accounts a happy man, and there was a good chance he'd stay so the rest of his days.

"I'm hungry," I said.

Minette was already sitting on the hutch, in her usual place by the Wedgwood teacup that doubled as her bed, her legs dangling over the shelf. "Are you angry with me, Kate?"

"I'm disappointed. Nothing I say gets through to you. I wish you'd understand that by exposing yourself like that, you put yourself in terrible danger. Not everyone has dementia, you know."

She lowered her head and looked at her toes as she swung her feet. "I wanted to help. You said I had fairy instincts but they were no good. I wasn't helping you and Emily. I *had* to help."

"Haven't you learned yet not to listen to me when I'm upset or worried?"

"But you tell me to listen to you."

"When I'm worried I say things I don't mean. I'm only human, after all." I gave her a smile and she stopped swinging her legs.

"Me too, Kate."

"And stop saying my pockets are tight."

"Yes, Kate. They're very loose. You could fit six fairies in them."

Laughing, I opened the fridge and dug around for easy leftovers. "Bread, cheese, and grapes. I'm not in the mood to cook, so they'll have to do."

"They sound stupendous!"

I swung around and looked at the hutch. Minette was always cheerful, always looking on the brightest side—and always encouraging me to do so. Months ago I might have said that was because she, like a dog or a cat or a frog, had no worries, but I knew now that wasn't true. She had lost her family and home in the terrible Olc. And as frustrating as life with her could be sometimes, she was now a friend, a dear companion, and I couldn't imagine life or my house without her.

"This evening we make plans to take back your forest, Minette, and we won't stop until it's yours again."

CHAPTER 17

A fter an early dinner, I phoned Emily. Had Laurence taken to his armchair with a good book this evening? If so, she needed to come to my house right away. There were plans to formulate. Then I made a cup of tea and took that and my laptop to the couch to do a little research. First, I looked up the word "Olc" to see if it meant something in the human world. To my surprise, it did.

I called out to Minette in the kitchen. "Is 'Olc' a Gaelic word?"

She floated like a nectar-drunk insect toward the couch. "I'm moving slowly and slowly, Kate. See?" Her wings vibrating but not flapping, she stopped in midair and drifted downward until she sat cross-legged on the couch back. "See? Slowly."

"You don't have to be so careful around me, Minette. I'm used to your supersonic speed by now—as long as you don't fly at my face. And I'm *not* angry with you. All right?"

She grinned like a child opening a present, eyes bright, shoulders bunched around her neck. "You're my friend, Kate."

"I *am* your friend. And so is Emily, and we're going to make a plan tonight. Now . . ." I gestured at the laptop.

"I love you even better than Emily, and I love Emily and her big pocket. But I love you more."

Was I that transparent? So childish and demanding that Minette felt the need to reassure me? "Thank you."

"You don't think so, but I do love you more. I want to stay with you."

For a moment I thought I might cry. Once again, honesty was called for. "I love you too, Minette, and thank you for saying you love me." I cleared my throat, willing myself not to start tearing up. "For now, when we're with Emily, you ride in her big pocket. I don't want you getting squished in my jeans. And when the weather's cooler, I'll wear sweaters with big pockets."

"Yes! That's it!"

"So now, let's figure out how we're going to win your forest back from Hacquetia and Thornbane. It says here that Olc is a Scottish Gaelic word, originally from Old Irish. The noun means evil, infamy, wickedness, and harm, and the adjective means evil, wicked, and corrupt, among other things."

Minette gazed with wonder at my laptop's screen. "The word is on the humans' computers."

"Without any mention of fairies, however."

She scooted across the couch back until she was almost touching my hair. "My great-grandparents were Scottish fairies."

"Really? Emily will be pleased to know you have Scottish blood. Her maiden name is Fraser—very Scottish. And so is MacKenzie of course."

"My grandparents and parents were born in the Smithwell Forest."

I nodded. "It's why your full name is Minette Plummery of the Smithwell Forest."

"But my parents never told me why they called the bad time Olc. I don't know what the word means, but they told me how to spell it. They taught me how to read."

"Where did Hacquetia and Thornbane come from?"

"From the Smithwell Forest. Thornbane was called Aramand before he decided to be evil." She laid a hand on my hair. "Emily is here now."

That phenomenal hearing of hers still amazed me. I rose, answered the door one second after Emily hit the bell, and then led her to the living room, recapping along the way my short talk with Minette. Emily circled the coffee table and took the couch's end seat, opposite from my laptop.

"How many evil fairies are we talking about?" she asked.

"There used to be seventy-six fairies in the Birch Street woods. Is that right, Minette?"

Minette took to the air, gliding at half-speed, settling atop a stack of books on the fireplace's hearth. "Yes, but the kind fairies have gone."

"Or died?" I said.

"Many died. I think . . ." Her eyes squeezed shut, her hands balled into fists as she concentrated. "I think there are about twenty very bad fairies left in the forest. I listened for them when we were there."

Stunning. "Twenty evil fairies in that little patch of woods across the street?"

"I never counted them, but I think I'm right, Kate. There were more of us before Olc, but they took us by surprise, and some of us ran away as soon as they killed my friend Pirabelle. My parents stayed with me, but they died protecting our tree. Hacquetia and Thornbane killed them." She abruptly twisted away from me, breaking eye contact. "The bad ones knew if they killed, we wouldn't know what to do and we would fly to safer forests. But I didn't want to leave Smithwell."

Emily was sitting in rapt attention, gripped with wonder, having trouble believing this alternate universe existed, let alone contained families and friends, good and evil, peacetime and wartime.

"All your memories are here," I said. "Of course you wanted to stay."

Emily crossed her legs and laced her fingers around one knee. "Holy guacamole. I mean . . . How do we even begin? I wish we could tell Laurence."

"No, no," Minette said, spinning back. "We must not."

"One day we might have to," I said.

"Not *now*," she said.

"But soon," I said. "We won't say a word until you let us, but you know you can trust Laurence, and you know he can help."

"If he doesn't have a heart attack first," Emily said with a gentle laugh. "When he sees Minette, he'll flip."

"So what do we do now?" I asked. "They live sixty, seventy feet off the ground in the trees. We need a way to draw them out and drive them off." Feeling the urge to keep my fingers occupied, I reached for my teacup and wrapped my fingers around it. "I don't want to kill any of them, but what if they attack Minette or us? You should have seen Hacquetia going like a green missile for my face."

"Minette," Emily said, bending toward the hearth, "I know this is a disturbing question, but what did the evil fairies kill other fairies with?"

"Emily . . . Emily, they used sharp thorns from the forest." Minette's voice shook. The very memory was terror to her.

I shuddered. "It's not only humans who are evil."

"There's evil everywhere," Minette said. "But there's good too."

"Well, now we *have* to do something," Emily said. "They can't go unpunished, and they can't be allowed to control the woods. Plans?"

My mind reeled. Trap them using bowls of maple syrup, like gardeners catch slugs with beer? Scream and shout, beat the bushes, threaten them, tell them their time is up? Send arrows into the trees, hoping to scare them into thinking we meant to kill them? All that would do is scare or even kill birds.

And then it hit me. It was risky, but it was a real plan that could yield real results. "We could tell Ignace Surette about them."

Emily gave me a look that said, *Have you lost your mind?* "Do I have to remind you that he's dangerous? Probably a killer? And anyway, he's long gone, back to wherever swamp he came from, I hope."

"I think I saw him driving his white BMW yesterday."

Emily gasped. "In Smithwell?"

"Downtown." I set my teacup on the hearth.

"That's when you got very quiet, Kate," Minette said. "I knew you saw something and didn't want to say."

"You're right. I couldn't quite make out his face, but I'm almost positive it was him. Same car, same gray hair." I drew a deep breath. "I've been telling myself it wasn't him, but who am I kidding? It was."

"Then he's a fool!" Emily said. "The police are still looking for him."

"Now that I think about it, he might have followed me. He turned to look at me just as he drove by. It was very deliberate—no coincidence."

"You're just now telling me this?"

"I set it on the back burner and tried to convince myself I didn't see what I saw. Minette, you told us that Olc brought the humans with nets and birdcages," I said. "How many humans?"

"Not many, Kate. Three, maybe. But I don't remember the Ignace Surette man back then."

"Have you seen humans hunting fairies over the past year?"

Her light brown hair swayed as she shook her head. "They left. When humans don't see us, they give up and go to another place to find us and trap us."

"Surette isn't concentrating on the woods across the street," I said. "He's searching all over Maine, and probably New England. That means he hasn't pinned down where the fairies live. He knows they're out there, but his hunting is hit and almost always miss."

Emily gave me a look of pure bewilderment. To her, this was not a bright idea. "And we're going to tell him where to look?"

"If he's back in town, what have we got to lose? We can bargain with him. I tell him exactly where the fairies are—right across from my house—he goes in, does what he needs to do, and then leaves me and the Birch Street woods alone. Minette, are you sure there are no good fairies left in those woods?"

"They're all gone. The evil fairies rule the forest and don't let the good fairies come home."

"Surette will return to those woods anyway," I went on, convincing myself as I continued to talk. "He's still hunting, and he's not going to stop. For some reason, he feels invincible."

"Maybe he is. He might be authorized to hunt. Sanctioned. Any crimes he commits in the process are null and void. Laurence thinks he's a French Canadian government spook."

"I'll tell him what Hacquetia looks like," I said.

"This could go very wrong," Emily warned.

She was right about that, but I couldn't see how we had a choice. Surette *knew* a fairy lived with me, and it was only a matter of time before he captured or hurt Minette. Last February he'd broken into my house in quest of her. He would not quit until I showed him a better bounty. "If we offer him nothing, he'll return to Smithwell over and over again. What do you think, Minette?"

She was sitting on the stack of books, gazing up at me, complete trust in her emerald eyes. Was I worthy of that trust? On many levels this was an insane idea. Even Emily and I weren't safe from Surette.

"The Ignace Surette must have a reason to leave us alone," she said. As she stood, her wings spread outward from her body and rose above her head. Her beauty—the face of a child with perfect ivory skin, pink and blush-colored wings, hair that shimmered in the light—still dazzled me. She shook her wings once, her body rising straight into the air, and then hovered near my face, feet together, toes pointed like a ballerina's. "Kate, even if he doesn't catch Hacquetia or her fairies, he will go to the Smithwell Forest many times and that will frighten them. After a while, they will be scared and find another forest."

"That's what I was hoping you'd say."

"Oh, boy." Emily gave me another one of her looks. This one said, *I'll play along, but I want you to know this is crazy.* "So how do we contact Surette?"

"He's following me," I replied. "Watching me. He might be watching my house right now. He still wants Minette."

Minette peeped involuntarily and covered her mouth with her hands.

"He will *never* get you," I said. "But we can hope he'll get Hacquetia and Thornbane."

Despite my plan being risky and a little nuts, I was suddenly filled with optimism. "Let's not waste any time. Emily, can you take a drive downtown?"

Emily phoned Laurence. Without giving an explanation, she told him we were heading downtown and might not be back for an hour.

"Is it okay?" I mouthed.

"He's deep in a book," she said, hanging up. "A thriller. He didn't ask me for details. Holy guacamole, Kate, this had better work."

Five minutes later we were in downtown Smithwell, making ourselves conspicuous by driving in lazy circles and then stopping for ice cream at Talbot's Creamery on Essex. Lingering in the parking lot, I licked away at my mint chip ice cream cone, searching for a white BMW—a car that stood out like a sore thumb in central Maine.

"This is how it feels to be a worm on a hook," I said. "Why don't you take Minette back to the car? Maybe if he drives by and sees me alone, he'll stop."

"You're confident he's watching?"

"He followed me yesterday. Chances are he's following me today."

Emily headed back to my Jeep and I wandered over to a picnic table and sat. The after-dinner crowd was streaming in now, providing Surette with people cover if he wanted to approach me. Everyone's attention was on children and ice cream, so as strange as his appearance was, he would fade into the crowd.

I was still working on my cone when Surette sat down beside me. His complexion was chalky, even in late summer, and his shoulders were as narrow and frail as I'd remembered.

"Well, my dear Mrs. Brewer," he began, in that oily, boot-licking voice of his, "I can't escape the feeling that you wish to speak to me."

Fighting to maintain my composure, I tossed my ice cream cone into a trash bin next to the table, looked him in the eye, and said, "Are you visiting Smithwell from Lewiston? Am I'm right in remembering you're from Lewiston?"

He grinned. Lord, when the man smiled he looked like a ghoul.

"*Très bien!* What do you wish to speak about, Mrs. Brewer?"

"Mr. Surette, I can't escape the feeling that *you* want to speak to *me*."

"I have always wanted to speak to you." He examined the nails of his left hand and began to pick dirt from under two of them. "But you never wished to speak. Or not for very long without throwing me unceremoniously from your house. Why were you waiting for me in this place?"

I shifted in my seat to face him, knowing it was vital I look tough despite my wobbling knees. Nothing less would keep me safe around a man like Surette. "I know why you're here, and I have a proposition for you."

"*Quelle surprise!*" He smoothed his long hair back from his forehead. "I'm intrigued. Do go on."

CHAPTER 18

Telling Surette I needed my walking stick to navigate through the ferns, brush, and fallen logs in the woods, I'd made him wait outside my closed front door. Emily left Minette in my house, and along with my walking stick I grabbed my pocket knife from a kitchen drawer and handed it to her. Then I asked her a second time if she was sure she wanted to go with me. Her answer was to phone Laurence and tell him we'd be in the woods foraging for berries until sunset.

We had forty minutes before it grew dark, I thought. Deep in the dense woods, we had twenty minutes at most.

Surette didn't trust me, of course. His eyes shot here and there, like pinballs in a machine, as we crossed Birch Street and started into the woods.

"You wouldn't betray our bargain, would you?" he asked me.

"Tell the police I took Ignace Surette to the woods to hunt for fairies? Not likely."

"They would ignore you or perhaps lock you up," he said with a bloodless snicker.

"Precisely." I kept telling myself that he already knew about fairies in Smithwell and I was only pinpointing the location for him so that, in keeping with our deal, he'd leave once he'd captured one or two. Or once his hunting had driven them from the woods. But then, I didn't trust him any more than he trusted me. "I've heard folklore about town. It seems that these fairies are greedy. Use their greed to lure them."

"Who told you this?" he asked.

"You're not the only one in Maine who knows about our fairies. There are books, and I've met people whose grandmothers taught them where to look for fairies. The lore is passed down through families."

"Ah."

"One fairy has made herself known to me. She's bold and nasty, for lack of better words. She's a bright, shiny green, rather like a hummingbird, and I think she makes her home in a maple tree close to the middle of these woods."

Surette looked skeptical. "Why would she make herself known to you, Mrs. Brewer?"

"She doesn't like me in her woods. And as I said, she's nasty."

He paused and gazed upward, studying the towering maples. "And so you don't mind me trapping her, *oui?*"

"I want my woods back."

"The problem is how to do that. How to use her greed against her."

"What do you do once you've captured them?" I wasn't certain I wanted to hear the answer.

"Oh, I would never hurt them. Oh, no, no. They're too valuable. Too precious."

"How many have you captured?" Emily asked.

He lifted his narrow shoulders. "None, unfortunately. Others have done so, but not me."

So Surette was incompetent. Suddenly I felt better about our whole arrangement.

"They're illusive," he said, starting off again, "and when you do see them, they're too fast." With his long legs, he dodged a clump of knotty vines.

"There's another fairy, also nasty," I said. "He's a sky blue color, with dark blue wings."

Surette smiled at me over his shoulder. "*He*, Mrs. Brewer?"

"Just a guess. It's the way he dresses."

"How many fairies would you say populate your charming woods?"

Lying to Surette brought me no sense of guilt. "Not many. It's a small wooded area with streets on both sides. It's surprising there are any at all."

There was a damp smell in the air that grew damper still as we moved farther into the woods, and in the distance, thunder rumbled a warning.

"It's getting dark and it's going to rain," I said.

Surette halted. "Stating the obvious, *non?*" He reached into his pocket and I gripped my walking stick with both hands. "There is no need for you to react like that, Mrs. Brewer. I simply want to show you this."

He extracted what looked like a thick silver pen, held it up, wiggled it, and snorted with satisfaction. "A powerful laser. Fairies are always looking, always. They can't resist. A colleague of mine says they drop like tiny rocks when this strikes them in the eyes."

First I reminded myself that the woods were full of nasty creatures who had brutally killed other fairies. Then I smiled appreciatively at Surette. "How interesting. I never would've thought of that."

"We shall see if it succeeds."

"But it *is* getting dark. Quickly. And I feel raindrops."

"All the better, Mrs. Brewer. Darkness befits creatures of darkness."

This was how Minette must have felt in the woods with Hacquetia and Thornbane on the loose, I thought. Scared, nervous, creeped out. "They're not all creatures of darkness," I argued. "Though the ones in these woods are."

Surette glowered at me for a moment then turned his attention to his laser pen, turning it over in his hands, fiddling with it. "What other fairies have you encountered?" he asked me.

"I've seen a few here and there. Never talked to them, obviously. I suppose I have an eye for them. My theory is, once you've seen one, you can see more. They eye knows how and where to look."

He chuckled.

Giving him my bare-knuckled tough-woman act, I stepped closer until I was two feet from his angular face. "And once you've seen them and tried to hunt them, whether or not you catch any, you're going to leave me and my neighborhood alone. Forever. You're going to keep our bargain."

He brandished his cherished pen. "But what if it takes weeks to lure and paralyze just one?"

"They're not going to hang around for weeks while you hunt them, and you know that, Surette. We agreed on two days, and you're going to keep our bargain."

He shook his head, seemingly amused by my naiveté.

"I have friends, Surette," I said. "Helpful friends."

He laughed. "*Mais oui*, I knew about these woods, but you confirmed the presence of fairies, and I thank you."

"Friends who know exactly who and *what* you are," Emily said.

"Is that so, Mrs. MacKenzie? Such as your husband? Everyone seems to be acquainted with him."

My pulse picked up. The colors of the setting sun had faded in the sky and thunder continued to rumble, moving ever closer. "You're a man on the run, Surette. A man with connections, but on the run nonetheless. Tell me this: Do you really think you're the *only* one with connections? Or the only one ruthless enough to use them?"

"Mrs. Brewer, please. No threats."

"I only threaten in return," I said. "You keep our bargain, and there's no need to carry out my threats."

He leaned toward me. I could smell something like greasy French fries on his breath. "Don't you dare. You have no idea the fire you are playing with."

It was no time to go weak. I steeled myself and planted a grin on my face. "Surette or Comeau, whatever your name of the moment is, our government connections are oh-so higher than yours. You've been allowed two days, no more."

Surette recoiled.

"I was sent to inform you. We knew you'd follow me. Your first day is rapidly coming to a close. If you don't leave tomorrow night, the boom falls."

He recovered his composure, but it was too late. I'd seen his fear. It was possible to threaten the man.

Emily came alongside me, smiled sweetly, and held her hand out, catching a few stray raindrops from the maples leaves, her silent and surreal movements beguiling Surette. Then she locked her eyes on him. "Mr. Surette. His name is Laurence. For starters."

You'd have thought she'd hit him with a rock. *Brava, Emily!* I was certain that, if we'd been standing in the light of day, I would've seen Surette's chalky face go paler still.

He went rigid and palmed his hair back for the umpteenth time. "There's no need. I'll keep to our bargain. I'm a man of my word."

Emily could never again tell me that Laurence was involved in "hotel construction." He was in construction like I was the Duchess of Kent.

I heard a voice from somewhere behind us, calling out above the thunder.

"That's Laurence," Emily said.

"You said it was just the three of us," Surette moaned.

"He doesn't know you're here today," Emily said. "He thinks we went berry picking, and we were supposed to be back by dark. We had planned to bring you here tomorrow—for your sake."

And then a second voice, a man's, called my name. I glanced at Emily. "Is that Rancourt?"

"You lied to me!" Surette hissed.

"I didn't tell him," I said.

"I told you it was getting late," Emily said, "but no, you had to go into your darkness spiel. Do you really think I invited my husband to settle his debt with you tonight? If I had, he'd be on your rear right now. Two inches behind you. He knows you, and rest assured he doesn't like you."

As Emily talked, I quickly weighed my options. I could trust Surette to keep his word, let him run, and not say a thing to Rancourt about him, I could let Surette run but tell the police he was in Smithwell, or I could tell Surette it was all a setup—there were no fairies in the woods, the silly man, and Rancourt was going to haul his rear off to jail.

"Three," I said aloud.

Surette made a face. "What?"

"You actually believe in fairies, Surette? You're right, we told Laurence and the police to follow us. It was all a setup and you fell for it."

Surette turned on his heel. "This isn't over, you—."

"No!" I raised my walking stick and hit him hard behind his knees.

He grunted, crumbled like the tall sack of bones he was, and hit the ground. "You broke it!" he cried, clutching his left wrist. "You broke it!"

"Laurence!" Emily screamed. "Back here—we need help! Keep coming!"

The weird and terrifying Surette, the man I'd dreaded for months, now writhed on the ground like a child and shouted out offense and indignation, his pride wounded almost as much as his wrist. In sixty seconds, Rancourt was literally on top of him, cuffing him and paying no mind to his injured wrist. The sheer weight of the detective made Surette's escape impossible.

Laurence grabbed Emily's shoulders, hugged her, looked at me and back to Emily, and then said something along the lines of "Berry picking—fat chance." I didn't quite catch his words because I was enjoying the sight of Rancourt yanking Surette to his feet and Surette's long gray hair, strung with leaves and other forest debris, swaying in his face.

As Rancourt marched him from the woods, Surette twisted back and spat at me, missing by a mile. Then his upper body went limp and he stopped struggling.

"Come see me tomorrow morning, Mrs. Brewer," Rancourt hollered.

Laurence was breathing hard, and not, I suspected, because the trim six-foot four-inch government operative was out of shape. "You two . . . I can't believe . . . Emily . . ."

"I'm so sorry, honey," Emily said. "I'll tell you all about it when we get back home." She glanced my way. "It's time you knew. Right, Kate?"

Laurence furrowed his brow. To forestall the questions forming in his mind, I jumped in. "Right now I need to go home. I hope they try that monster for murder."

"Rancourt might charge him," Laurence said, "but that's Rancourt. He's honest and doesn't give a rip who's connected to what. I'd be surprised if Surette stands trial, and even more surprised if he's convicted."

"You're joking," I said.

He shook his head. "We haven't heard the last of him. I tried to tell you both a few months ago. He's dangerous."

"So are you, honey." Emily wrapped an arm around his waist. "You'll understand why we did this when I explain."

"Wait a second," I said, "why was Rancourt here?"

"He wanted to tell you Angie Palmer will probably be charged with manslaughter," Laurence said. "Not first- or second-degree murder." His breath, I saw, had slowed. "I saw him at your door when I took the trash out. He thought you'd want to know."

"That was good of him."

"I said I was worried about you two, and he came with me. It *was* good of him."

Laurence was calming down, his fight-or-flight instincts dissolving, but I knew Emily was going to have a devil of a time explaining why we were in the woods. He wouldn't believe her. At first he might suspect she'd lost her mind. "Did Surette drop his laser pen?" I asked her. His pen would be partial proof of Surette's intentions.

"Why did he have a laser pen?" Laurence asked.

Emily and I scanned the forest floor where Surette had been standing when I'd hit him. In the near-darkness, I spied a silver tube. "Got it!"

"Again," Laurence said, "what's the deal with the laser pen?"

I handed it over to him, told Emily to call me later, and headed back through the woods. "I have to get home, guys. See you later."

MINETTE SAT ON MY kitchen table, sipping from her tablespoon of maple syrup. She leaned in, drank, sat back, savored the taste, leaned in again. She deserved a treat, partly because Hacquetia and Thornbane had not been vanquished, but also because Emily was, at that very moment, telling her husband that a world even he, spy that he was, could not imagine existed did indeed exist. Across Birch Street *and* inside my house. They would be over soon, I'd told her.

Minette had taken it well. Better than I'd expected. "It has to be done, Kate," she'd said, "and I like Laurence. He won't tell on me, and I won't have to hide from him anymore."

"He'll never tell on you, I promise. And now we can ask him to help rid the woods of those evil fairies. Maybe he can make use of Surette's laser pen."

Emily could never again pretend that her sweet husband wasn't a spook, I thought with a smile. She could no longer laugh and change the subject. She *knew*, and the proof of her knowledge was that she'd used Laurence's reputation to shock Surette, another man with odd connections.

When Minette had her fill of syrup, I told her what Rancourt had said about Angie Palmer being charged with manslaughter. "She might serve only two or three years," I said. "And I'm sorry you'll never see the terrestrial orchids from her greenhouse, but I'll look for one at Foley's Nursery."

She smiled up at me, her childlike face beaming, her green eyes shining. Minette had never been reluctant to show joy or pleasure—unlike many humans I knew—and the older I got, the more I valued that generosity of heart. It was evidence of an open soul, of a human, or other creature, not afraid of ridicule, willing to cast self to the wind and be vulnerable. Maybe I'd found her, or she'd found me, so I could learn to be a little like her.

"When Jack Palmer goes to a nursing home, and he will soon, would you like to pay him a visit?" I said. "He'd love to talk to his magic friend."

"Can I?"

"I think we can manage it."

"Yes, Kate!" She shot two feet above the table, tucked her legs, and did a somersault mid-air. "I like Jack! Make it soon!"

Also by Karin Kaufman

SMITHWELL FAIRIES COZY MYSTERY SERIES

Dying to Remember (Book 1)

Dead and Buried (Book 2)

Secret Santa Murder (Book 3)

Drop Dead Cold (Book 4)

Dastardly Deeds (Book 5)

Counterfeit Corpse (Book 6)

JUNIPER GROVE COZY MYSTERY SERIES

Death of a Dead Man (Book 1)

Death of a Scavenger (Book 2)

At Death's Door (Book 3)

Death of a Santa (Book 4)

Scared to Death (Book 5)

Cheating Death (Book 6)

Death Trap (Book 7)

Death Knell (Book 8)

Garden of Death (Book 9)

Death of a Professor (Book 10)

Still as Death (Book 11)

Grim Death (Book 12)

TEAGAN DOYLE MYSTERIES

Chasing Angels (Book 1)

Call of Chaos (Book 2)

CHILDREN'S BOOKS
(FOR CHILDREN AND ADULTS)

The Adventures of Geraldine Woolkins (Book 1)

More Adventures of Geraldine Woolkins (Book 2)

Springtime with Geraldine Woolkins (Book 3)

Book of Tales: Volume One (Book 4)

ANNA DENNING MYSTERY SERIES

The Witch Tree (Book 1)

Sparrow House (Book 2)

The Sacrifice (Book 3)

The Club (Book 4)

Bitter Roots (Book 5)

A Note to Readers

"The things I believed most then, the things I believe most now, are the things called fairy tales. They seem to me to be the entirely reasonable things. They are not fantasies: compared with them other things are fantastic."
~ G.K. Chesterton

"He does not despise real woods because he has read of enchanted woods; the reading makes all real woods a little enchanted."
~ C.S. Lewis

When I was very young I longed to believe in magical creatures, lands, and phenomena. Talking animals, enchanted forests, dragons and fairies, wormholes in space. All the fantastical and as-yet hidden wonders of God's creation.

And like most adults, a part of me still longs to believe in those things. So I created Minette, a fictional character who lives in what just might be a nonfictional world. (There are whispers . . .)

After all, who's to say there are no fairies? Human beings, as Minette points out, have limited vision. "Just because you never saw me before doesn't mean I don't exist." she says. "There are all kinds of things you don't see."

As I wrote the first book in the Smithwell Fairies series, though, there was one thing of which I was certain: If fairies do exist, they're not the roly-poly cherubs or vampish nymphs they're most often pictured to be. They are God-created creatures with a magical dignity all their own.

Minette would agree.

If you were entertained by *Dasterdly Deeds*, please consider leaving a quick review to help spread the word. Every review, no matter how long, is greatly appreciated!

Newsletter Signup

For the latest news on the Smithwell Fairies Cozy Mystery Series and other Karin Kaufman books, sign up for her newsletter at KarinKaufman.com.

Made in United States
Orlando, FL
13 August 2023

36055599R00104